Mostly the HONEST TRUTH

Jody J. Little

HARPER
An Imprint of HarperCollinsPublishers

Library of Congress Control Number: 2018948779
ISBN 978-0-06-285249-6 (trade bdg.)

Typography by Jenna Stempel-Lobell
19 20 21 22 23 PC/LSCH   10 9 8 7 6 5 4 3 2 1
❖
First Edition

For Mom and Dad

Day One

The Road to Three Boulders

There were no signs along the highway posting how many miles to Three Boulders.

Believe me, I was looking real hard.

For a long while I bounced in the cab of Officer D's rusty red pickup, cruising along Highway 24. Then, without warning, Officer D cranked the steering wheel to the right, gripping it with her man paws, and roared onto a dirt road. I pressed my bandaged hand tight against my belly. That jostling and bouncing made it ache pretty bad.

Officer D must have noticed me grimacing because she slowed the old truck a bit and asked, "Your hand sore, Jane?"

"Nah, I'm fine," I lied, squeezing it a little tighter, holding in the achiness. "Are we there yet?" I asked.

"Just a few miles up this road."

"You got a McDonald's in Three Boulders?" I asked. "I'm a little hungry."

That was the honest truth. It felt like ages had passed since I ate that crummy ham sandwich at the hospital.

Officer D laughed at my question. She had a low, deep, belly kind of laugh, but it wasn't loud like Pop's laugh. I used to tell Pop that his laugh scared my ears, but I didn't really mind. I missed his laugh already.

"No McDonald's, Jane. In Three Boulders, we eat all our meals at Noreen's dining hall, and Noreen is one fine chef. I believe she's making mac and cheese tonight."

"A dining hall? What's that?" I tried to picture eating in a hallway. Me and Pop usually just ate on the kitchen counters or in the living room watching TV.

"Our dining hall is like a cafeteria," Officer D explained.

"Like at school?" I hoped that wasn't the case.

"No, much better. You'll see tonight." Officer D focused her green eyeballs ahead. "Watch for deer and jackrabbits, Jane. There's a lot of them out here."

We zigzagged along the dirt road, avoiding the potholes. I wanted to take my mind off all the pain in my hand, so I pictured a good me-and-Pop time from just a few months back. It was a Saturday night and we were longboarding at Jefferson Park. We'd circled the park once, then Pop pushed me on the swings. Then we'd circled again. It was like the best looping carnival ride you could imagine. We coasted around for hours until it started getting dusky. Pop could have boarded until the coyotes howled. That's what he always told me. But he could tell I was getting tired. He reached down and scooped me up in his arms. *I got you, Jane Girl.* And I knew he did.

The road was less bumpy now as the pickup traveled along the carved grooves. There were no animals, unless you counted the bugs splattered on the windshield. The only things I saw outside were tall brown grass, a bunch of gray rocks, and pine trees lining the road.

"How come you live all the way out in the boonies?" I asked. When I met Officer Doris D. Dashell a year ago, I just figured she lived in Willis, like me and Pop.

Officer D tapped the steering wheel with her thumbs a few times before answering. "Being a police officer can be stressful, and Three Boulders is a calm place. It's a family-like community."

"You must have a huge family," I said. The Nelsons were a huge family. They were my second foster family. They had seven kids of their own, and they still took me in for twelve whole days. The front door of that house never stayed shut with all those kids. I spent most of my time there parked on the couch in the living room, where they all played video games. I just watched that door open and close. Every time, I hoped it was Pop, coming to take me home.

Officer D shook her head. "The folks in Three Boulders aren't related to me, but I think of them as family."

My family was Pop. That's all. Me and Pop. Pop and

me. Two perfectly matched socks. I liked it that way. So did Pop.

"So these people are sorta like your foster family."

"I suppose."

"Have you brought a foster kid to Three Boulders before?"

"No, Jane, I have not."

"So why did you bring *me*?" The old truck sank into a pothole and flung me against the door. I winced and held my hand tighter.

"Well . . ." She glanced out her side window, maybe digging in her brain for the right words. "I thought since we know each other, you might like being around a familiar face." She dug in her brain again. "And you might like some of the folks here."

"Does your sorta foster family know I'm coming?"

The corner of Officer D's mouth lifted a bit, a cop smile. "Things happened fast last night and this morning, so I only had time to let a few folks know."

She sure had that right. About things happening fast, I mean.

I didn't even say goodbye to Pop last night. One minute he was on the kitchen floor with me, holding my arm and mumbling mishmash words, and the next thing I remember it was morning, and I was propped up in a bendy hospital bed. A nurse wearing purple scrubs was bandaging me up, and Officer D was there, telling me I'd be going home with her that afternoon. Her face was all scrunched up, worried like.

I was only worried about Pop. He had to get better. Worrying made my hand throb even harder.

"Those folks you talked to, do they know *why* I'm coming to Three Boulders with you?"

She let out a long exhale before she answered. "Jane, part of being an officer of the law is that I'm required to maintain confidentiality."

That was good news to my ears. I knew *confidentiality* meant you kept your mouth shut and didn't blab. There were certain things I was real confidential about.

Officer D was nothing like my past foster people. I couldn't picture her ironing my hoodies and my underwear, or offering me extra pink blankets each night like Mrs. Dubois had. But just in case, I *did* ask her, "Are you going to comb my hair every morning?"

"Don't you comb your own hair, Jane?"

"Not every day. I only have to comb it once a week, after I shower."

Officer D laughed at that.

"Mrs. Dubois, my last foster person, sat me in her kitchen every morning for twelve whole days and combed and yanked my hair into two braids," I explained. "Mrs. Dubois was kind of like a hair artist. She showed me pictures of the fancy braided dos she once gave her daughter. Those braids looked like sculptures on the top of her head. I told her that regular braids would be fine for me. I figured having a braided statue might make me tip right over. Besides, my longboard helmet wouldn't fit over the top of a hair sculpture."

Officer D laughed again. "Jane, I don't even know how to braid hair."

"I bet you don't need to comb yours either," I added.

Officer D rubbed her dark, cropped hair and grinned. "That's true."

I was actually relieved she didn't comb or braid hair *and* that she had all that confidentiality stuff. No one needed to find out anything about me or Pop or my hand. I would stay in this Three Boulders place for the usual twelve days, and then I could go home. Home to Pop, where everything would be good again.

Yep, twelve days in rehab for Pop. Twelve days in a temporary foster home for me. We'd already done it three times before, but this fourth time was going to be the last. I had made sure of it. That's the honest truth.

"I'd like you to meet someone when we arrive. She'll be pleased to show you around. Her name is Gertie Biggs."

"Gertie?" I quickly shoved those other thoughts to the back of my brain. "What kind of name is that? When you say it, it sounds like you're hurling. Listen." I sucked in my stomach, rolled my shoulders forward, and let out a belchy-like sound, "Gerrrrrtie."

I knew that wasn't very polite, but sometimes I couldn't help myself. Pop said words flew out of my mouth like a lava-spewing volcano. I looked at Officer D, expecting her to reprimand me like a cop or a foster person should, but she didn't.

"Gertie's a good kid. She's eleven years old, same as you, and sharp as a Taser zap. Anything you want to know about Three Boulders, Gertie can tell you. I think you two will get along quite well."

That was fine and all, but there was no point making a friend for just twelve days. I would longboard as much as I could and watch TV. That's how I planned to spend my time in Three Boulders. I'd be counting these twelve days carefully. Counting was something I was pretty good at.

I pulled Pop's orange stocking cap down over my ears and stared out the side window where there were fewer bug splats. We drove around a corner and I saw the first signs of civilization since we'd turned off the highway: ten cars parked in a grassy field. Officer D pulled up next to a silver sedan and shut off the engine.

"All right. Let's go."

I opened the truck door and slid out, slamming it behind

me. I looked around. Other than the parked cars, there was nothing but pine trees, dirt, rocks, and shrubs. There were no houses, no buildings, no light posts, no streets.

"*This* is Three Boulders?" I asked.

"This is where we park and hike. There's no road for cars into Three Boulders. Come on. I'll carry your stuff." She flung the black plastic garbage bag shoved full with my things over her burly shoulder.

"How far do we have to hike?"

Officer D shrugged and headed toward a faint path into the pines. "About a mile or so," she answered without turning back to look at me.

With my good hand, I snatched my longboard out of the bed of her truck and jogged a bit to catch up with her.

What in the world kind of crazy place was this Three Boulders?

Gertie Biggs

My forehead got all sticky with sweat trudging up that tree-lined path behind Officer D. She moved like she was chasing some criminal in front of us. I stepped over poky rocks and vines and swatted at bugs that swarmed around my nostrils.

I remembered a summer afternoon a few years back, before we lived in Willis. Pop had just bought a new barbecue with his tips from the Brunch Beanery. He grilled us each three hot dogs. We sat on the tiny deck of our apartment eating them. Bugs were swarming around my face and fingers just like they were now. I swatted and spat at those mini pests. Pop laughed at me. He said, *Jane Girl, you can't let life's little annoyances get to you. Learn to ignore them. Like me.* And then he crossed his legs, yogi-style, and he chomped on his hot dog.

Sometimes Pop's advice was hard to follow. I yanked

off his stocking cap and waved it in front of me, but those stupid bugs just wouldn't leave me alone.

Finally, Officer D stopped in front of a big log cabin with a porch wrapped around three sides. I dropped my longboard and let out an exhale of relief.

"Welcome to Three Boulders, Jane," she said.

I looked up the dirt road to my right and saw maybe twenty or so smaller cabins with green metal roofs, hardly bigger than toolsheds. On my left was a field of grass with a baseball diamond and backstop. Behind me was that long, bug-filled path that led back to the parking lot.

Did Officer D mean that *this* place, this log cabin, and lousy gravel road was Three Boulders? *This* was my foster home where I was supposed to live for twelve days? This wasn't even close to being a town. This was more like a campground.

No, *this* was boonieville.

"Is this your house?"

"This is Noreen's dining hall." Officer D tromped up the creaky porch steps. "I live in a room upstairs."

This was nothing like my other foster places. The Yarbers had a normal house with a grassy yard and a fence. The Nelsons had that big old house with the slamming door. Mrs. Dubois lived in an apartment where I had to climb stairs to the third floor.

But this old cabin was something from a story, like the

one where the little old woman made a gingerbread man who ran off into the trees yelling, "You can't catch me!"

I climbed the five porch steps of that big log cabin, and there, sitting in a rickety rocking chair next to the door, was the oldest dude I'd ever seen. His brownish and blotchy skin blended right into the wood of the cabin. He had black plastic glasses propped on his lightbulb nose. His ears stuck out like coffee mug handles. Resting across his lap was a long shotgun. His pointy finger was stuck right inside the trigger hole. And he was sound asleep.

Or maybe dead.

Something about that ancient dude gave me a little tingle down my arms, making my bandaged hand tweak with pain. I put the orange stocking cap back on my head and gave him another long glance, checking out his wrinkles and the skinniness of his chest.

Officer D put her finger to her lips to silence me. She pulled open the screen door and motioned me inside.

Noreen's dining hall was a big open space like the gym at my school. There were three rows of long tables with blue-checkered cloths. Those tables spread clear across the wood floor, which made it look like a restaurant.

And, man, did it smell good, like fresh waffle cones at the Dairy Maid. I sucked in a big nose-full of that goodness.

A bunch of grown-ups sipping coffee sat around one table. Every last one of them turned their heads when we entered. They scanned me from the top of Pop's orange stocking cap to the toes of my skate shoes, and their voices all rose at once and kind of formed a buzzing cloud of noise around me. I heard some words through the buzzing like *welcome* and *hey, there* and *who's this, Doris?*

These folks must be the sorta foster family Officer D mentioned. There sure were a lot of them, way more than the Nelsons and their seven kids. I wasn't too sure about being around so many adults. Adults made me kind of nervous, except for Pop. Adults asked a lot of questions which I didn't always like to answer.

I stepped back and felt Officer D's chest firm against my back. Her supercop senses must have felt my nerves because she gave those adults some sort of silent signal and the buzzing died away, and they went back to their coffee.

Officer D gave me a little push forward and guided me toward the second row of picnic tables. There, with her back to the adults, was a girl in a sunshine yellow T-shirt. Her face was snowman white and her light brown hair frizzed out in a big wide triangle. She had a heaping stack of spiral notebooks in front of her and was writing furiously.

"Gertie Biggs," Officer D said.

The girl let out a short gasp, dropping her pen. "Oh! You're here already."

"Sorry to disturb your work," Officer D continued. "Please meet Jane Pengilly."

I reached toward the girl and squeezed her right hand, strong and firm, like Pop taught me. I kept squeezing until her brownish eyeballs grew wide and her mouth frowned a bit, which was my cue to let go. Pop taught me that too.

"Sit, Jane. I'll let you two get acquainted." Officer D patted my back. "I have a few things to take care of, but I'll find you before supper."

The bench creaked as I pulled it away from the table to sit across from the girl. I hid my achy hand under the table and asked, kind of in a whisper, "Is your name really Gertie?"

"My real name is Gertrude."

Gertrude was a horrible name, even worse than Gertie. Some parents just did not think carefully when naming their children. Pop said he gave my name lots of thought. He said Jane was strong and sensible and no one would ever make fun of it or pronounce it wrong.

"I think I'll just call you G."

She looked puzzled. "No one's ever called me G."

"Then I'll be the first."

I was about to start asking her questions about this Three Boulders place, like why were there no paved roads and what cable channels did they have, when I noticed a half-eaten piece of pie sitting next to her. My stomach started growling at me, so I asked, "You gonna eat that?"

"Shh." G put her pointer finger to her lips, ignoring my

question. She leaned back just a tad, turning her ear ever so slightly toward the adults at the table behind her.

I leaned forward too, but all I heard was grown-up mumbles. Adults never seemed to have anything interesting to say, except for Pop. His brain was filled with essential life-learning wisdom, like how to get bubble gum out of your hair and how to change the wheels on your longboard.

"I knew it," G said in a low voice. She picked up her wooden pen and scribbled something down in one of the notebooks.

"What did you know?"

"Gerald and Emma Carter *are* leaving Three Boulders. My parents told me it was just a rumor, but I didn't believe them."

G's hand flew across the paper as she spoke. I kept staring at the pie.

"Are you going to eat that?" I asked again.

She didn't answer, but she pushed the plate toward me.

I picked up the fork and shoveled a whopping bite into my mouth. That pie was filled with fruity yumminess, and the crust was nothing but fried butter and flour. I slowed my chewing down, savoring that bite. "This is—"

Before my words could tumble out, G shushed me again and checked out for another eavesdropping session.

"No way," she whispered. "Did you hear that? It sounds like Timmy Spencer and his mom might leave also."

"So? People move all the time. I do."

"But they love Three Boulders." G was still whispering.

"Pop and me loved Walport, but *we* still moved. We kind of had to, though. We packed only what could fit in Pop's Datsun."

G gave me a long questioning glance but then began writing in her notebook again.

I scooped another bite of pie between my lips, but this time my taste buds sent me a different memo, maybe more like a warning. I scooped another forkful and held it up to my nostrils. I sniffed. I sniffed again.

This pie had alcohol in it.

My brain filled up with a memory of Pop from last night, his yucky breath . . .

I quickly set the fork on the plate and pulled the stocking cap down my forehead. I didn't want to think about last night. I was done thinking about it.

I was done eating this pie too.

I felt a little stabbing pain in my hand and wrist, and I kind of wanted to go find Officer D right then 'cause she was the only familiar thing around me.

I looked across the table at G. The adults stood up, gathered their things, and headed toward the dining hall door.

"Drat." G tapped her pen on the table, frowning. "I need to figure out what is going on around here, why people are leaving."

"Aren't you supposed to show me around?" I asked.

Her triangle head shot up, and she flashed a huge smile. "Right!" She slapped the notebook closed and dropped it on the pile. "I'll investigate this leaving business as we go." She shoved all the notebooks in a backpack resting on her left side. "Where do you want to start? The softball diamond? The church fire pit? Cabin row?"

I sat back just a bit. She was bursting as though this place was a great amusement park, and she couldn't wait to take me on every ride.

What could she possibly be so excited about?

The Tour

"Do you play softball?" We were on the dining hall porch now. The rocking chair where that ancient dude had sat was empty.

"Softball? Only in PE class," I said.

"Oh. That's too bad." G glanced at my bandaged hand, and I tucked it inside my hoodie pocket.

"We have a big game coming up next weekend. You probably know how good Officer Dashell is. If they had professional softball teams, she would be all-American. I'm sure of it."

"She's never mentioned softball to me."

G continued. "Officer Dashell holds most of the batting records in Three Boulders *and* the most consecutive games without an error."

"Is that good?"

"Good? It's great!" She leaped in the air when she spoke.

"She'll figure out some position for you. Everyone plays. That's a Three Boulders law."

"Law? There's a law making people play softball?"

But G didn't respond. She just marched down the porch steps and turned left. I followed.

"There's the softball field." G pointed.

I gazed at the rickety bleachers and softball diamond. A bearded man on the pitcher's mound hurled a ball at a runty kid who swatted it into the grassy field that was neatly mowed in diagonal stripes.

"That's Preston Farmer pitching. He's our garden coordinator. The little kid is Timmy Spencer. Timmy's the current push-up record holder."

"What are you talking about?" My brain was whirling with all G's information.

"He set the push-up record three months ago on record night."

"Record night?"

G explained, "We have record night once a month. You can challenge any current record holder to a duel. We have a hot-dog-eating champion, a knitting champion, a Hula-Hoop champ, and tons more."

Now I was just plain dizzy. Record night? Push-up champion? Knitting champion?

I pinched myself just to make sure I wasn't in some faraway dreamland.

G led me up the gravel road. We passed a white wooden fence circling a garden and my nose was attacked by a gust of poop smell. I covered my nostrils with my good hand.

"That's our community garden. You'll get used to the smell," G said. "I'll show you that later. I want you to come to my cabin."

Holding my nose tight, me and G trudged up the gravel road that was now separating the little log houses, the ones I'd noticed when I first arrived. The logs were shiny, like someone had actually polished them, and the roofs were green metal. I bet they made an awesome sound when it rained. Some cabins had flowers growing near the front doors and others had colorful flags swaying in the breeze. As weird as this Three Boulders place was, these people took good care of it.

G pointed to every cabin as we walked. "That's where the Steins live, and over there is the Landaus. This one is Mr. Farmer's, and here's the Donalds. . . ." She kept rattling off the names in her cheerful tour guide voice.

"And this is my house." G stopped at the last cabin in the row, identical to the others except for a chalkboard sign right at the doorway that said *Monday: All students meet at the fire pit at 10:00 a.m.*

"Come in. You can meet my mom and dad."

I followed her inside. It was like stepping into that gingerbread man storybook house. A black woodstove was running even though it was May. Two comfy chairs and a plush couch with blue fur pillows filled the front room. I looked at the shiny log walls lined with photos of G and her triangle-hair head at different ages. In every photo she wore a long flowered skirt, just like she wore now.

"Nice, isn't it?" G beamed.

It was nice. It made me feel kind of warm inside, but a little sad too. Me and Pop didn't have photos like that. He said we didn't need pictures when we were always together. Sometimes Pop forgets that we aren't always together.

"Where's your TV?"

"We don't have one. No one does."

That stunk.

No paved roads meant no longboarding, and no TV meant twelve days of nothing but counting and waiting.

Some of that warm feeling oozed away.

"We do have movie night once a week. Mr. Landau sets up his DVD player and projector in the dining hall. It's fun. We all bring in blankets and pillows," G gushed.

One of the doors inside the cabin opened and a man stepped in the room. His forehead was tall and kind of shiny red, which made him look friendly to me. "You must be Jane." He moved toward me. "Doris mentioned that I'd have a new student. I'm Mr. Biggs, Gertrude's father. I'm the Three Boulders schoolteacher."

"Teacher? I have to go to school?" It probably wasn't the

best thing to spew out right after meeting him, but this bit of info was a newly paved speed bump. Officer D never said one thing about school. Now I wasn't feeling warm at all.

"School is a requirement for kids in Three Boulders, Jane, just like everywhere else," he said. "You may find that you like the way we do it here."

I doubted that. I was not a fan of school. Pop told me my problem was that I had TBS, twitchy brain syndrome. That meant my brain kept wanting to jump around to different places, but in school they don't like it when your brain does that. In school, your brain has to stay calm. Just like when Pop starts to drink alcohol after months and months of nothing but coffee and milk. My brain has to stay calm then too.

Right then a woman walked into the front room. "This is my wife, Mrs. Biggs."

Mrs. Biggs gave me a smile. She had hair bigger and wider than G's. She stepped toward me and gathered me in her arms for a hug. Her hair frizz tickled my face. I didn't much like being hugged by strange people. I only liked Pop hugs.

"Welcome, dear girl. It's so nice to have a new face in Three Boulders," she said, still holding me in her arms, my achy hand and wrist smooshed into her belly.

A knock on the cabin door freed me from her grasp. Mrs. Biggs opened the door and in stepped the ancient dude from the porch.

I guess he wasn't dead.

He hunched over slightly, his left hand gripping the handle of that shotgun, the gun barrel thumping on the floor. His gray eyeballs pierced me, and I felt another tingle just like I had on the porch.

"You must be Jane." He reached his hand toward me.

I wasn't too excited about shaking that wrinkly hand, but I knew I had to because it was important to be polite while I stayed here with Officer D. *Be polite and don't cause trouble in your foster home, Jane,* Pop always said. *Trouble might keep us apart longer.*

So I shook his hand strong and firm just like Pop taught me, and that ancient dude squeezed my good hand in return. Man, he had a wicked grip for being close to two hundred years old.

When he finally let go, he said slowly, "You're a skinny thing."

I didn't think that was a real welcoming comment. I couldn't help that I was skinny. Pop was skinny too. And this ancient dude was not one to talk. His bones weren't exactly packing a lot of meat.

"Eleven years old, correct?" His voice was crackly and deep.

Officer D must have told him my age. What else had she said to him?

I nodded, and he nodded back, slowly.

"I look forward to a visit soon, young Jane." He thumped his shotgun cane on the cabin floor, but then looked past me. "Ernie and Helena, may we speak? I need to share some news with you."

"What news?" G said. I could see questions practically written on her face.

"This is not for the records right now, Gertrude," Ancient Dude answered firmly. "You and Jane run along. Dinner will be served soon."

G's shoulders slumped forward. She paused for a long second.

"Go, Gertie," Mr. Biggs insisted.

I opened the cabin door, but Ancient Dude called my name and I turned back around.

"Jane, I'm glad you're here," he said.

Well, I wasn't so glad.

The Interview

"Something is going on around here. I've got to figure it out," G said. She was marching me back down the gravel road. "People are whispering. People are leaving. Old Red is talking to my parents in private. What do you think it could be?"

"How in the world am I supposed to know? I've been here for two hours. All I know is this place is *really* weird."

G gasped. She spun around and faced me. "Maybe it's you."

"What's me?"

"What's going on in Three Boulders. Maybe it has something to do with you." She was peering at my face like she held one of those scientific magnifying glasses.

"That's the craziest thing I've ever heard. How could I have anything to do with whatever is going on?"

G let out a big huff. "I need to think about this. Come on."

She walked a ways farther to a little side path that ran between two of the cabins. At the end of that path was a big log that someone had shaped into a bench.

I was glad to sit down. I pulled off Pop's orange stocking cap and set it on the bench. I needed to let some heat out of my brain and some ache out of my hand. The May breeze felt cool drifting through my hair. On the backrest of the bench, names were carved in capital letters.

"This is the Three Boulders Kid Bench," G said. "Every kid who's ever lived here is listed. You can carve your name. I've got a pocketknife in my pack."

"I don't live here. I'm just visiting."

I scanned a few names. I found *Gertrude* right away, carved in perfectly formed letters. I saw *William*, *Hank*, *Millie*, *Megan*, *Timmy*, *Lenny*, and *Jerry*. I traced *Jerry* with my pointy finger. That was Pop's name. Seeing his name made my hand throb harder.

"Hey, G, what's the deal with that ancient guy? Is he, like, the king of Three Boulders or something?"

That question snapped G out of her thinking place. In fact, it seemed to perk her right up. "That's Old Red Norton, but he's not a king. Three Boulders is not a monarchy. It's a democracy."

Those big words got lost in my brain, and G must have noticed because she said, "A monarchy is where one person makes all the laws. A democracy is where everyone gets to vote and agree on laws. But Old Red does own all the land, so he's sort of in charge." She unzipped her pack and reached inside, pulling out a blue notebook and opening the front cover.

"Here." She pointed. "This is Old Red Norton."

I took the notebook and read what it said:

Red Elijah Norton
Years in Three Boulders: 70
Age: 91
Jobs in Three Boulders: founder and mayor
Family: wife, Eleanor (deceased).
          Daughter, Florence (deceased). Grandson
Special skills: hunting, wiring, citizen mediation
Softball position: umpire

"Seventy years? How can anyone live in one place that long?" I asked.

"Because he likes it here." G looked at me like I was crazy for asking such a question.

I tried to picture Old Red as a younger man, sitting on the dining hall porch in that chair, rocking back and forth, shotgun on his lap.

I glanced at the journal entry again.

"Why don't you have his grandson's name?" I pointed to the space right after the word *grandson*.

G shrugged. "Old Red didn't tell me what it was."

I turned some pages in her journal and read another entry:

Officer Doris D. Dashell
Years in Three Boulders: 7
Age: 42
Jobs in Three Boulders: peacekeeper
Family:
Special skills: law enforcement, weapons maintenance
Softball position: first base

"Why is her family section blank?" I asked.

"She wouldn't tell me anything about them."

That made me a little sad. Officer D was a solo sock. Her match was swallowed into the clothes dryer's stomach.

Well, I could be her foster kid for twelve days—a white sock paired with a navy sock.

But that's all.

I flipped through the journal a bit more. "Why do you have this?"

"It's my notebook of the People of Three Boulders. I interview everyone who lives here. I should add you."

It was real clear to me that this frizzy-headed girl was not letting go of me living in Three Boulders. Maybe if I had bigger words to use, she would get it.

G took the blue notebook from me. She shuffled through the pages until she found a blank section. "Okay, name and age?"

I didn't actually want to be interviewed for her journal, but I also needed to be polite like Pop always said. Besides, I could always make stuff up. I was good at that. "Jane Pengilly, age eleven."

Truth.

"Jobs in Three Boulders . . . well, we'll have to leave that blank for now," G said. "I'm sure Old Red has something in mind for you."

G moved on. "Family?"

"My pop, Jeremiah Pengilly," I said. "Most people call him Jerry. You can write that down. I just call him Pop."

"And your mom?"

"Don't have one. Write deceased."

Truth again.

G shifted on the bench and looked at me. It was the same look I got from everyone, especially foster people, when I told them I didn't have a mom, like they were doing everything in their power not to lean over and hug me, and tell me how much I must miss her. But I don't miss her.

Truth. Mostly.

"It's okay," I explained. "She died when I was born, so I don't remember her at all, and that's just fine 'cause I got Pop, and he's the best pop in the world for me."

Honest truth.

But inside my brain I thought about how I had Pop *most* of the time. There were some times when Pop was next to me, but he wasn't *with* me. There was a brown paper bag between us on the couch, and inside the bag was a bottle of disgusting, smelly alcohol. Those were bad me-and-Pop times, and those times led me to my foster families, but foster families don't count. They were temporary, like twelve-days temporary. Blood relatives were *real* family. That was what Pop always said.

G looked down at the journal. "Brothers and sisters? Grandparents?"

"Nope and nope. I'm an only kid, and my grandparents are dead. I mean deceased. Make sure you write *deceased*. That looks very official." I tapped on her journal.

G wrote the words down. "Special skills?"

"Longboarding, for sure. I'm real good at talking too and playing solitaire and old maid. I'm a good counter and adder, but not a good minuser and divider. Don't write that down. I make good grilled cheese sandwiches. I know the entire menu at McDonald's. Should I keep going?"

"No, that's probably good." G filled two lines with her special wooden pen, and then she asked, "Why did Officer Dashell bring you to Three Boulders?"

This was where I figured the interview should end. I didn't want to tell G about last night and why I was here with Officer D. I would maintain confidentiality.

I changed the subject. "Is your job in Three Boulders the town spy?"

G's mouth flopped open. "I'm *not* a spy. My job is town record keeper."

"So more like an eavesdropper?"

"I don't . . ." She tapped her pen on the journal. "Okay, when the need arises, I do have to use my keen hearing ability to decipher dialogue, perhaps not meant for me to hear."

More big words. This girl was smart.

"I think that's called eavesdropping, G." I was pretty sure I was right.

G grinned at me, and then she quickly covered her mouth, holding in a giggle. "I still prefer town record keeper."

She pulled all the journals from her backpack. "Let me show you. Black is for Laws of Three Boulders. Blue is People of Three Boulders. Red is Daily Events. Green is the Community Garden Log, and purple is the Duty Log. I write everything down that happens. That's my job."

I picked up the red journal and read aloud. "'April 30: Millie Donald missed school due to a sore throat. Lettuce and carrots were planted in the community garden. Alan Stein began pitching practice for the softball season.'"

I slapped the journal closed. "Do you *like* this job?"

G took the red journal from my hand. "It's the best job in Three Boulders."

More weirdness. I had never heard of a place where kids had jobs like this.

"Who reads those journals?"

"Old Red looks at them every week."

"So he knows everyone's business here?"

"Pretty much."

Well, crud.

I definitely had to *do* the right things and *say* the right things, 'cause if the honest truth slipped out, I feared that these next twelve days could turn into twelve weeks, or twelve . . .

My brain couldn't even consider that.

Jane, Pop had said last time, before I went away with Mrs. Dubois, *it's only twelve days. You mind your business and I'll mind mine, and we'll be back together faster than you can bomb Applegate Hill.*

Applegate Hill was my first big longboarding hill. I was eight years old. Pop and me lived in this town somewhere in Washington. I was scared to bomb that hill because it was majorly steep. My whole body shook, but Pop was there, and we were having good me-and-Pop days—months, actually. *I got you, Jane Girl*, he said. Pop rode slow right alongside me, grabbing my hand when I wobbled, picking me up when I fell.

Me and Pop. He picked me up when I fell. I picked him up when he fell. Those were *our* jobs.

I leaned forward and peered over my knees at a tiny, crawling ant, thinking about that hill—that good me-and-Pop time. If I could bomb that hill, I could mind my own business and get through these next twelve days in boonieville.

Even with all the weirdness.

Even with my achy hand.

Day Two

Officer D's Room

I dreamed I was with Pop. We were plopped on our brown vinyl couch, smooshed together, watching his favorite news show. He had a bowl of popcorn in his lap. He shared it with me, Pop-style. Him tossing pieces in the air. Me trying hard to catch them in my mouth and mostly missing. I grabbed the bowl and took a turn. Pop caught every piece I put in the air. When I flung it too far, he just bounced the kernel off his arm or knee and it shot right into his mouth. He'd shout out "boo ya" and slap me a high five. He was a champion popcorn-catching athlete. I was in the middle of a standing ovation for Pop when I felt a tap on my shoulder, jolting me awake.

"Time to get up, Jane."

I sat up, quickly realizing I wasn't watching the news with Pop. Pop was in rehab. I was here in Three Boulders with Officer D, my newest foster person. I rubbed the sleep goobers out of my eyes.

"Sorry about that couch, Jane. I know it's a bit lumpy."

I coughed to clear my sleepy throat and said, "It was fine. I've slept on worse couches than this at other foster homes. The couch at the Yarbers' smelled like old squishy potatoes."

I looked around Officer D's room, wondering again why she lived *here*, in this tiny room above the dining hall in boonieville Three Boulders instead of Willis.

"Officer D," I said, "your room reminds me of this motel room that Pop and me lived in for a few weeks. Except that it doesn't have itchy bedspreads and stiff pillows and ugly paintings of sailboats."

"Thank you, Jane." She sat down next to me on the couch. "We need to put a clean dressing on your wound." She lifted my bum wrist and gently unwound the old gauze. I cringed and sucked in my breath. It felt like she was peeling off large chunks of flesh.

She squinted at all the redness, twisting my arm slightly side to side. "Is it hurting?"

"Just a little," I said softly.

Not the honest truth.

"Need one of those pills?"

I nodded.

She brought me a little pill and a glass of water and

lifted my arm again, rubbing white goop all over my hand and wrist. "I'll try to be gentle, Jane."

The very first time I met Officer D, she fixed one of my wounds. It was about a year ago. I was testing out my longboard on our new street in Willis, and I crashed and burned near Miss Tally's house. I trudged home with a skinned knee and elbow, and when I got there, Officer D was on our porch talking to Pop with a bag of groceries in her arms. When she saw my road rash, she went to her cop cruiser and snagged a first-aid kit, then cleaned my wounds and slapped on bandages, just like she did now.

She continued to come by our house, maybe once a month, always with groceries, which was good 'cause Pop didn't earn a big paycheck. Sometimes she and Pop whispered together outside on the lawn. Pop never told me what they talked about. Officer D with her confidentiality probably wouldn't tell me either.

"It looks like you and Gertie got along well yesterday," she said.

"She gave me a tour of this place," I said. "There's weird stuff here." I thought about the softball field; the stinky garden; all the tiny cabins; the record night; and that ancient dude, Old Red. "Officer D, did you tell Mr. Norton about me?"

She gave me a stare but didn't answer.

"He knows about Pop, doesn't he? About him being in rehab."

She secured the fresh gauze around my wrist with a piece of tape but still didn't answer me.

"Me and Pop shouldn't be anyone's business but me and Pop," I said firmly.

"Jane," she finally spoke, "you must understand that it would be nearly impossible to bring you to Three Boulders without sharing a little of your story with Red Norton."

I lifted an eyebrow.

"Red has lived here for years. It's his community essentially. He wants to understand why someone would want to live here, or why they might *need* to live here awhile."

I pretty much wondered the same thing. Why would someone want to live in a place with no roads and no TVs and no McDonald's?

"G told me he owns this land," I said.

"That's correct."

"So he's rich, like a billionaire."

"Owning land doesn't exactly make you rich." Officer D rose from the couch and grabbed her holster lying on her bed.

"Well, it seems like he could do better than this." I waved my good hand in circles, indicating Officer D's room.

"I happen to like *this*, Jane." She waved her hand, just like I had. "The quiet simplicity of Three Boulders is comforting. I'm not a fancy person."

Me and Pop weren't fancy people either. I wasn't being rude on purpose.

Officer D didn't seem upset with me, though, because she buckled her holster and kept on talking. "Since it's his land, he has certain guidelines for letting folks live here. He wants to know their stories. And once they are here, he expects folks to follow the laws."

I wondered if I met Old Red's guidelines. I wondered if I'd be able to follow all the rules and not cause trouble. I wasn't always good about that.

"This place is just weird. All of you living up here in the middle of nowhere. I miss Pop."

"I know." She put her hand under my chin and lifted it gently. Big, burly Officer D didn't seem like a parent person, but the way she raised my chin reminded me of Pop. He always did the same thing.

"Can I call Pop today?"

"You know you can't, Jane."

"Will *you* talk to Pop today?"

She moved to her dresser and picked up a lint brush, swiping it down the sleeves of her cop shirt. "Possibly."

"If you talk to him, tell him I'm doing good and that my hand is just fine. Tell him to watch our shows because I don't have any TV. Tell him that I miss him but that we have only eleven more days. Okay?"

"If I see him, Jane, I'll tell him. Now get dressed. It's

pushing eight o'clock, and we want to get to breakfast before the bacon is gone."

She sure had that right.

"*And*, it's your first day of school in Three Boulders. You don't want to miss that."

She sure had that wrong.

The Laws of Three Boulders

I followed Officer D down the stairs to the dining hall. Three Boulders folks were already seated and stuffing their mouths with pancakes and scrambled eggs. Last night, I'd learned that meals in Three Boulders were like one enormous picnic. Everyone sat at the long wooden tables, passing enormous bowls of food around, always from the right to the left. Me and Pop never did that. We just scooped our food right out of the pan off the stove. At the Nelsons', I had to sit at a table with all their kids and pass food. Mrs. Nelson was a bad cook, though. Her tomato soup was cold, and she put mayonnaise on canned pears. I pretty much starved at that foster place.

Officer D was right about the food here in Three Boulders. It was the best I'd ever had.

That was the honest truth.

I scanned the people at the tables and saw G sitting

with her mom and pop. She was wearing that sunshine shirt again. So were most of the other kids.

I made my way toward her, and she scooched over so I could slide onto the bench next to her. Mr. and Mrs. Biggs said good morning and passed the pancake plate. I took four, watching the steam ghosts rise from the big doughy disks. With my good hand, I carefully added butter and warm maple syrup and dug in. Pop would sure love these.

"Jane, we're starting a new project in school today," G said. "It's a nature project."

"That's right," Mr. Biggs chipped in. "I'll be telling you all about it this morning. Nine o'clock by the fire pit."

I swallowed a bite of pancake goodness. Why did they have to ruin my breakfast by mentioning school?

"Do I really have to go?" I asked, because maybe the rules were different if you were only staying a few days, like me. My TBS was kicking in just thinking about school.

"Of course you do!" G put her fork down. "It's actually written down in the Laws of Three Boulders. I can show you."

She reached behind her and grabbed her backpack, pulling out her black journal, labeled Laws of Three Boulders. She flipped forward a couple pages and handed me the journal, pointing to law number 26: All children under the age of 19 must participate in school activities as directed by a qualified adult.

"She's right, Jane," Officer D said, taking a slurp of coffee. "I'm going to buy you a shirt in Willis today so you'll have the right uniform too."

So those sunshine shirts were uniforms. I guess it was better than the uniforms all the Nelson kids had to wear to their school, those green polo shirts and ironed khaki pants. Maybe I could just wear the shirt and *pretend* to be in school. I could pretend real good for the next eleven days.

Officer D began chatting with Mr. Biggs and another man about the softball diamond, but I got distracted when I saw Old Red slowly making his way around the tables, hunching over his shotgun cane, talking to folks, one at a time. G was watching him with her hawk eyes as well. I could almost see her brain churning, figuring out what he was saying. When he came toward us, he nodded at me. "Good morning, young Jane. I trust you slept well."

I remembered my dream about watching TV with Pop, and I thought this might be a good time to suggest a satellite dish and televisions here in boonieville, but Officer D spoke first. "She slept like a baby, Red. Lumpy couch and all."

"Wonderful." He gave his shotgun cane a big thump on the floor. "Doris, a word with you before you leave for Willis this morning?"

"Certainly. I'll meet you in a bit." She gulped one last mouthful of coffee and turned to G. "Gertie, I trust you can show Jane all the ropes today?"

"Of course, Officer Dashell." G smiled.

Mr. and Mrs. Biggs rose too, waving goodbye, and pretty soon me and G had some space around us. I didn't plan to leave anytime soon, especially if leaving meant going to school, so I scooped scrambled eggs onto my plate and turned a page in the Laws of Three Boulders journal. There was a law about stealing, a law about feeding wild animals, and a law about what time families had to be in their cabins. There were lots of laws about softball games. Softball seemed to be a major topic of conversation around this weird place.

Then I read law number fourteen: There is to be no alcohol consumption, nor possession of alcohol in the community boundaries at any time.

That put a little spark inside my brain. That law wasn't being followed. I remembered the pie I ate yesterday.

I nudged G with my elbow. "Hey," I said, pointing to law number fourteen. "This law is being broken."

"What are you talking about?"

"That pie I ate yesterday. It had alcohol in it."

"What?" G said loudly, and then she glanced around the table. A few folks were looking at us. G whispered, "How do you know that? Do you drink alcohol?"

"Of course not!" That was a Three Boulders law I intended to follow way beyond my twelve days here.

Then I pretty much blurted out the honest truth, but real quiet, so only G could hear me. "I know because it smelled like the stuff my pop sometimes drinks."

"But that can't be true. In Three Boulders *everyone* follows the laws, even Chef Noreen. Officer Dashell makes sure of it. So does Old Red."

"Well, that pie had liquor in it, and just because you have a law, it doesn't mean that people will always follow it." I knew that was true. Not everyone in the world was a law-abiding citizen like Gertie Biggs.

G scanned the big room with her worried face. She leaned in toward me and said, "About two years ago, a man named Marty Muldoon lived here. One night he came back from Willis and was staggering up the road, and then he just passed out right in front of the dining hall. Officer Dashell saw him. She yanked Mr. Muldoon to his feet, slapped cuffs on him, and schlepped him all the way down the path and back to Willis. He wasn't allowed in Three Boulders again." G paused and sat up straight. She held up the black notebook. "These laws are what keep our community strong. There is no alcohol here."

"Maybe there's a different law for cooking?" I suggested.

"There's not a different law. Alcohol is *not* allowed." She gave one solid nod of her frizzy head.

All this yummy food was definitely waking up the

smartness in my brain, because an idea came to me right then, an idea that just might delay school and all the work that came with it.

"Okay," I said. "Let's go find out."

"What do you mean?"

"Let's search the kitchen and see if we can find the alcohol."

"But we can't," G whispered. "We have to get to school. And there will be people in the kitchen cleaning up after breakfast, so we can't be rummaging around for mysterious alcohol."

Pop's words, *stay out of trouble*, whizzed through my brain. But how could searching for something cause trouble?

"Fine. We'll wait 'til they're done cleaning," I suggested. "As the Three Boulders record keeper, don't you think you should find out?"

G was silent, but I could tell she was thinking hard. I'd only known her for one day, but in that one day, I'd learned that her eavesdropping, law-abiding nature had to find the truth, the honest truth.

And I was right because she squinted at the silver watch on her wrist and then said, "Okay. We'll search. They should be done in the kitchen about 8:40. I'll *prove* there's no alcohol in Three Boulders, and then we'll still make it to the fire pit by nine."

The Kitchen Search

When G's watch read 8:39, we took a soft dirt path around the dining hall to a red door at the back. G put her ear against the door, using her fine-tuned hearing to listen for voices. After a few moments, she nodded to me, turned the knob, and pushed the door open. I entered the kitchen behind her. There were three sinks the size of bathtubs, four refrigerators taller than Pop, and two wide ovens stacked along the walls. In the middle of the room were long, shiny steel countertops, with open cupboards above, filled with blue and yellow dishes. Swinging metal doors on the far side of the room led to the dining hall. "Cool. It's like a restaurant."

"Shhhhh." G put her finger to her lips. "Be quiet."

I ran my good hand along the smooth steel counters. "It's so clean. I could eat right off these counters. I could eat off the floor!"

G tiptoed across the black-and-white tiles, her long flowered skirt shifting from side to side.

"Where's all the food?"

G waved and I followed her into a little room lined with open shelves. "This is the pantry. See for yourself. Spices and baking goods here. Canned foods on that shelf. Dry goods on this one. Root veggies in the floor bins." She pointed to each section of the room. "See? No alcohol."

"She wouldn't store it out in the open if it's not allowed. She'd hide it. It's probably in a paper bag."

I moved to the canned food shelf and lifted cans, setting them on the floor.

"Don't touch anything! Noreen will know if something is out of place."

G grabbed the cans off the floor and carefully placed them back on the shelf, facing all the labels forward.

"We're just looking. We're not stealing."

G exhaled. She glanced over her shoulder and wiped her hands on her skirt.

"Come on, help me." I reached for a box of cereal, the nutritious wheaty kind that Pop never bought. I opened it and grabbed a handful of flakes, tossing them into my mouth. "Yuck. These aren't any good." I accidentally dropped the box, and cereal scattered on the floor.

"Be careful, Jane!" G bent down and swept the cereal into a pile with her hands.

"Sorry. I'll take care of it." I pushed the pile of flakes into one of the dark corners with my skate shoe. "You keep looking."

G sighed, but she tiptoed to a shelf and pushed aside a clear jar filled to the rim with homemade cookies.

"Don't look there."

"Why not?" she whispered back.

"She wouldn't hide alcohol behind cookies. Cookies are something people want. Something they would pull off the shelf to eat."

"How do you know where Noreen would hide something? You don't even know her."

"Trust me. I know things like this." I moved aside cans of water chestnuts and artichoke hearts. "She would hide it where people wouldn't notice it." I stepped back and scanned the little room. "Like on those top shelves."

Setting my foot on a low shelf and my good hand on a higher shelf, I pulled myself up so I could see what was stored way up high.

"Jane! Be careful. I don't think these boards—"

Crrrrraaaack!

Oops. That didn't sound good.

I jumped down and peered at the shelf I had stepped on. It sagged like a wide *V*.

"You broke Noreen's shelf."

"It's not broken," I answered quickly, pushing up the

shelf from underneath. "It's just cracked a bit. I think I can fix it."

But each time I pushed up and let go, the shelf fell back into that *V* shape. If Pop was here, he could fix this in a jiffy.

"I need to find something to prop it up," I said.

I squatted. Maybe there was something on the floor I could use. I saw a wire basket filled with red and yellow onions, and I scooted it out of my way. I got down on my knees and leaned over. It was dark below those shelves, but I noticed something glimmer, deep in the back. I reached in and felt a glass bottle. I stretched to grab it with my good hand and pulled it out.

"Hey. Look what I found." I held the green bottle up toward G.

"What?" She moved away from the cracked shelf and grabbed the bottle from my hand. She shook it, listening to the liquid slosh around. "It's probably a special syrup."

"Open it."

G untwisted the cap and stuck the open bottle under her nose. "Ugh!" She spun the cap back on and thrust the bottle back into my hand. "That's not syrup."

I managed to take off the cap with my good hand, and sniffed for myself. I was all set to say I told you so, but then I saw G staring at the bottle. Her pale face looked like she was watching a ten-car pileup on the freeway.

"It's not a big deal," I stammered. "I bet she just uses it for special things . . . like pie."

"What do we do?" G panicked. "Noreen's not supposed to have that!"

"We could throw it out," I suggested. I did that once when I found one of Pop's bottles. I dumped it all into the toilet and flushed five times to be sure it was gone. It didn't work though. He had a different bottle the next night. He never even mentioned the other one.

"Noreen will be kicked out of Three Boulders, like Marty Muldoon." G gasped.

"Let's just put it back."

"But . . . I know it's here. I have to document the broken laws. I'm the town—"

But G stopped, because just then we heard the whoosh of those swinging metal doors. G spun and moved out of the light from the doorway.

Someone was coming.

I still held the bottle of alcohol in my hand. There was no time to put it back where it belonged, so I stuck it in the first hiding place I saw: G's backpack. I unzipped the top, shoved the bottle in, and zipped it back up.

I wasn't sure G even noticed. She waved her hand, furiously motioning me to stand against the wall, in the shadowy part of the room. If someone walked in and turned a one-eighty, we would be spotted, but there was nowhere else to hide. We hunched down. G put her hands over her mouth. I was quiet. Sometimes I really did know how to keep my mouth shut.

I heard a deep, crackly man's voice. Old Red Norton.

My hand and wrist began to throb.

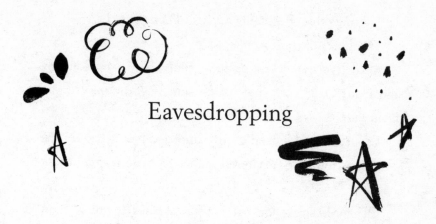

Eavesdropping

"I'll make my official announcement tomorrow," Old Red said.

"Good," another voice responded. I knew this voice too. Officer D.

"I've already spoken to Gerald, Preston, Amelia, Ernie, and Helena."

G pulled her hands away from her mouth. Her brow wrinkled and she leaned closer to the open doorway, assuming her professional eavesdropping posture.

"It's the right decision, Red," Officer D said. "But I know this is all happening sooner than you thought it would."

I could see G's lips asking "What?"

"I just want it all to be okay," Old Red said.

"So do I," Officer D answered.

There was a tiny pause and then Old Red asked, "How is she, really?"

"Remarkable. Resilient," Officer D answered.

"And her injury?"

Wait. Were they talking about me? There was a big long sigh from Officer D, a sigh that said *Well, let me tell you about that.*

G turned and looked at my bandaged hand. I could see a big question mark plastered on her face, even in all these shadows.

Officer D spoke for real. "I think it's hurting more than she's letting on."

How would she know that? Besides, I just told her this morning it was fine.

Old Red didn't respond, but I heard a big thump that made both me and G flinch.

Officer D said, "I'm meeting up with a few folks from social services tomorrow morning regarding Saturday's incident."

Wait.

I did *not* like hearing that news. Every time Pop went to rehab, ladies from the social services would come talk to me. Social services people were nosy. They asked too many questions. I would tell the ladies about me and Pop being matching socks, but they would just smile at me and start asking more questions, and then suggesting I stay with my foster people longer. They never understood how much *I* needed Pop. How much *he* needed me. Being away from

Pop for twelve days was enough. I swallowed a bit, trying to push away all the worries sloshing around my insides.

"Have you learned more about what really happened?" Old Red asked.

"No."

There was another pause. I pictured Officer D in her crisp cop uniform, arms across her burly chest, rocking back and forth on her feet.

"Has he spoken?"

"Just a bit."

"And?" Old Red asked.

I felt my jaw drop like an egg splatting in a fry pan. They were talking about Pop now. Officer D should be talking to *me* about Pop, not this ancient dude. This was none of his business. My insides were simmering now. A part of my brain was telling me to march out of this pantry and tell them to stop talking about me and Pop. G must have heard my brain too because she put her hand on my knee, bracing me down.

"I don't think he remembers much right now," Officer D said.

A picture from that night leaped into my brain: Pop, flat on his stomach, his face smashed into the couch cushions.

I hugged my burning hand into my belly and pushed my back hard into the wall behind me.

"Well, Doris, I think being in Three Boulders for a spell

will be good for her. There's nothing like this place: fresh air, good food, community, and a change of pace."

G bobbed her head.

Change of pace is *not* how I'd describe this place. It was more like a change of planet.

"I need to get in to work now," Officer D said. "I'll update you this evening on this business, and as for your other situation, I think folks will understand."

"I hope so. Three Boulders means a lot to everyone here."

And then the conversation ended. I heard the whooshing doors again, and the thump, thump, thump of Old Red's shotgun cane.

G sat like a boulder. Her mouth was a gaping black hole.

So was my brain.

Saturday. Pop on the couch. My hand. Those social services people. Officer D and Old Red talking about me.

Something felt real bad about all this.

School in Three Boulders

Me and G waited in the dim pantry. We just sat, side by side, each of us puzzling over what we just heard.

G spoke first. "They were talking about you and your pop, weren't they?"

I nodded, wondering what Pop had said, or what he hadn't said.

"Is your pop in trouble?"

"He'll be fine," I said. But on my insides I was crossing my bones, hoping for that to be true.

G stared at my bandaged hand. I could tell she wanted to ask me about it. I spoke quickly before she could. "What do you think Old Red's announcement is?"

"I don't know, but something is changing around here." She let out a long exhale and gazed at my face like she still wondered if weird things were happening because of *me*.

Whatever Old Red's announcement was, it couldn't have anything to do with me.

G looked at her watch. "We're late for school. We have to go."

I was hoping she might forget about school.

We left the kitchen and passed through the empty dining hall, where all the tables had been cleared of dishes and wiped clean. G picked up the pace when we got outside, leading me across the gravel road and down a narrow path that led to some sort of fire pit encircled with logs. I hadn't seen this place yet.

The Three Boulders kids in their sunshine shirts sat in a row on one log, all eight of them, clipboards in their laps. Mr. Biggs stood in front of the fire pit, talking. He raised one eyebrow when he saw us, giving us that teacher-knows-all look. I got that a lot. "Nice of you both to show up. You're tardy."

"Sorry, Dad," G said.

But I didn't apologize. I didn't even want to be here. My brain was too full of worries to squish in extra words and numbers.

Mr. Biggs continued. "We'll collect bark samples of each tree and determine . . ."

G picked up two clipboards, handed me one, and then we sat on the log behind the row of sunshine kids. G set her backpack between her legs, unzipped it, and gasped.

"Gertrude?" Mr. Biggs asked.

G zipped up her pack, lightning-bolt quick, and she glared at me. Her look pierced me down to my pinkie toenails.

"What's wrong? Did a bee sting you?" asked Timmy Spencer. He bounced on top of the log. I figured he had TBS too, only his was twitchy *body* syndrome.

"I'm fine," G said, exhaling. But my toenails were still feeling her eyeball glare. "I just scratched my hand on something. Sorry, Dad."

That was a pitiful explanation. She could have come up with something way better, like maybe she nicked herself with her pocketknife, or maybe there was a rat making a home in her pack.

I, of course, knew exactly what had happened. She had seen that bottle of alcohol I had shoved in her backpack. I avoided G's face.

Mr. Biggs continued his teaching. "We'll investigate the medicinal benefits of the foliage . . ."

I scratched a note on the paper held down by my clipboard: *Sorry, G.* I pushed it toward her.

She scribbled back: *You're not supposed to write notes during school.*

I wrote: *I always write notes. Notes are better than doing school stuff.*

She wrote: *What am I supposed to do with you-know-what?*

I wrote: *I'll figure it out. Don't worry.*

"We'll also do some photography," Mr. Biggs continued. "Mr. Landau has brought two macro lenses for our use. . . ."

G glanced at her pop and then grabbed my clipboard and wrote another note: *I can't stop thinking about Old Red's announcement.*

I couldn't stop thinking of different things, but I wrote back: *Maybe he's bringing in cable TV.* I added a happy face.

G didn't respond with a note, but I could see her eyes rolling circles.

Mr. Biggs was still talking. "You may work alone or with a partner. Your choice, but I expect quality befitting your abilities."

The sunshine kids began unclipping papers and shoving pencils in their packs. They rose from the log.

"What's going on?" I asked.

"It's time to start the project," G said. "You can be my partner."

"School is over?" I folded up our note and stuffed it in the side pocket of my cargo shorts. "No spelling tests? No division? No silent reading?"

Mr. Biggs must have heard me because he said, "You can read anywhere, Jane. You don't have to be in school to do that. I'll check all your spelling on the paper you'll write for this project. Gertie will help you too."

"So, that's all?"

Mr. Biggs smiled. "I can give you some long division to work on if you'd like."

I shook my head firmly. "No thank you."

"Mr. Biggs only meets with us for a little bit each day," a blondie girl said.

"The rest of the day you work at your own pace," another blondie chirped.

G pointed at the blondies. "Jane, meet Millie and Megan Donald."

Twins. I would never be able to keep them straight, but I liked what they told me.

It felt like my twitchy brain was getting a long restful nap. School in Three Boulders would be a breeze.

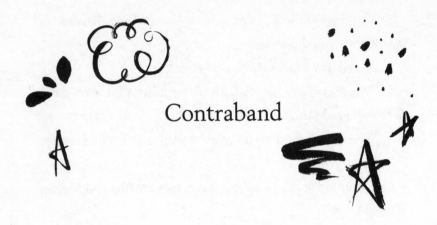

Contraband

G and I left the fire pit area and returned to the kid bench where we had sat yesterday. I yanked a prickly leaf off the bush right behind the bench. "I'll keep this for our first flauna sample, G."

"It's flora, Jane. Flora and fauna, not flauna. *That* is Oregon grape. It's everywhere in Three Boulders."

"Can you eat these berries?" I asked, holding them in front of G's face.

"No," she said. "I can't focus on this project right now, Jane. There's contraband in my backpack. Old Red has some major announcement, and *now* my dad is acting weird."

"He is?"

"He usually gives us month-long projects. This nature project feels short, like it will only take us a few days. I don't get it." G rubbed her hands on her thighs, smoothing her flora skirt.

I wasn't going to try to figure out Mr. Biggs. Short project. Long project. I didn't really care. All I knew was that I didn't have to be seated at a little desk all day in a dusty classroom with those number-two pencils that never have erasers and stacks of math worksheets in my unfinished work folder. I liked this Three Boulders school. I couldn't wait to tell Pop about it.

"Why did you put that bottle in my backpack, Jane?"

"I had to put it somewhere. I didn't have time to put it back where it belonged."

That was the honest truth.

"What am I supposed to do with it?" G asked, a tiny screech in her voice.

Before I could answer, my ears heard the crunchy sound of footsteps on gravel. Coming toward us were two sunshine kids, a shaggy-haired boy and a small girl with a crooked walk.

"Gertie," the boy said, "are you okay? You were acting weird back at the fire pit."

G pressed her triangle hair behind her ears, but it just sprang back out. "I'm fine. So is Jane." She elbowed me, which I figured meant to keep my mouth shut.

"Hi," the boy said to me. "I'm Loam Moonbeam."

"*Loam* means 'soil,'" G explained.

I gazed long and hard at that boy. "Your name means dirt?" I blurted out, shaking my head.

That was just plain wrong. You don't name a kid after dirt.

G gave me a stink eye, but the shaggy-haired boy didn't seem bothered.

"I like to think of loam as rich, earthy soil," he said. "This is my sister, Dandelion. We call her Dandy. She doesn't talk." He put an arm around her shoulder.

Great. Dirt and a weed.

The poor girl even looked like a weed, tilted and kind of wilty on the edges, sort of like God didn't get something quite right with her.

Weed girl smiled. She held up both hands, spreading her ten fingers out stiff and wide. Then she lifted one bare foot, wobbling side to side, showing me her dirty toes.

"She's telling you that she's fifteen," Loam said. "She's small for her age. Probably won't get much bigger."

Then, carefully, weed girl began moving her piggy toes, first the big one, then the pinkie toe.

"Now she's telling you that I'm twelve," Loam translated.

That made me like this weed girl, bad name and all. Pop showed me that same trick on my eleventh birthday. He said I had grown out of fingers to show my age and now I had to add my toes.

Weed girl sat down on the bench right next to me. She touched my orange stocking cap and then clapped her hands together. Maybe that was her way of telling me she liked my cap. Sometimes it might be real convenient not to be able to talk like this girl. Social services people could ask me questions all day, but they wouldn't get one single answer.

That would be convenient for sure.

Loam asked, "What are you guys up to? You're never late for school, Gertie."

"We're not up to anything," G answered, quicker than necessary. She was clinging on to her backpack so tightly her arms were quivering.

"What's really in your backpack? A dead squirrel?"

Dandy scrunched up her nose.

"Journals," G answered.

"I know that, but you have something else in there too. You can tell me. I'm your friend, Gertie."

G went mute, so I blurted out, "Actually, you could help us out, Loam. You see, we found a bit of contraband."

"Jane!"

"Really?" he said, his face turning pinkish. I couldn't tell if he looked excited or guilty.

"Show him, G."

"No! Are you completely crazy?" she snarled.

Maybe sometimes I was, but I didn't really want to be saddled with this bottle of alcohol either. If anyone found out we had it, it might be serious trouble for me. I needed someone else to deal with it. I knew Dandy wouldn't say anything, and something about this dirt boy made me think that he wouldn't say anything either. Maybe it was his shaggy hair that he didn't bother combing. Like my straight hair. Or how his sunshine shirt was dingy. Like my gray hoodie. Or maybe it was how he took care of his sister. Like I helped take care of Pop. My brain didn't really know, but I felt like this kid could keep a secret. Like me.

"You always help me with my homework, Gertie. Let me help you," Loam said.

"It's okay, G. Open your backpack," I said.

G did not look pleased, but she super slowly released her clingy grip and unzipped her backpack.

Loam leaned over and peered inside, then he stood up tall and let out a long whistling exhale. "That's some real contraband for sure. Where'd you find it?"

"On the floor behind the bin of onions in the kitchen pantry. Will you put it back for G?"

"For me? I wasn't the one who took it!" G's eyeballs shot a few invisible bullets at me.

"I'll handle it," Loam said. "Don't worry."

And he leaned over again, untucking his shirt from his jeans. He reached into G's backpack and slid that bottle right under his shirt, slick and speedy, as good as a street magician.

"You don't have to worry about this contraband again. I'll take care of it, right, Sis?"

Weed girl clapped her hands and off they went.

G gave me another eyeball glare. "He better put that back, Jane."

I couldn't help but smile. I thought my plan was perfecto.

Contraband problem solved.

A Note to Pop

That night as it got dark, I sat on the lumpy couch in Officer D's room. She had gone down to the kitchen and brought me back a mug of hot cocoa filled with mini marshmallows. I'd never had a foster person who'd done that for me. Ms. Dubois made me hot tea once. She called it something like *chameleon* tea and it tasted bad, just like I imagined a dirty chameleon might taste. I didn't finish it.

"Good cocoa, Jane?" Officer D asked, slurping on her own mug of marshmallow yumminess.

"The best," I said.

Honest truth.

"I told you Noreen was a great cook. I don't know how she does it. I only know that everything she makes is quality."

Well, I knew something about Noreen. Something

secret. It sure seemed like there were a lot of secrets in Three Boulders.

"Tell me about your day. What did you think of school?"

I was feeling real comfy right then, sitting next to burly Officer D with our mugs of yummy cocoa. I was just about to spew all the details of Mr. Biggs's nature project when I remembered sitting in the kitchen, eavesdropping on Officer D and Old Red. I remembered how they talked about me and Pop and Saturday night. A tiny bit of anger grew in my gut, and I didn't want to chat about school with Officer D. I didn't want to show her the leaves that were stuffed inside my cargo shorts pocket or the plant book G had loaned me.

Officer D had broken all that confidentiality that she told me she was required to maintain.

So instead, I asked, "Did you see Pop today?"

I had learned that Officer D had three faces. There was her I-mean-business cop face, the one that practically shot bullets out her pupils and made people follow her orders. Then there was her question face, the face she used when she didn't quite believe you, the face that made the stubby hairs on her head stand up taller. That was the face she gave me this morning when I said my hand was doing just fine. And her third face was her worry face, or her almost-like-a-parent face. That was the face I saw when she arrived at my house Saturday night, the same one she wore at the hospital as they bandaged my hand and wrist.

Right now, she gazed at me with her question face. "I saw him, but I didn't speak with him."

"Oh." I took a gulp of cocoa. "Did anyone else talk to him?" I had to be careful what I asked, but I also had to know if he had talked to those nosy social services people.

Officer D put on her cop face. "He's undergoing some interviews, Jane, but not with me." She set her cocoa mug down and leaned forward. "Whatever happened Saturday night requires some sorting out." She paused. Her cop face remained. "Do you want to talk more about that night?"

"No," I said. I did *not* want to talk about it.

That night was over.

But I *did* want to talk to Pop.

"Officer D, is it okay if I write a note to Pop? A get-well-soon note?" I added.

"That seems like a fine idea."

"You won't read it, will you?"

"I will not." She rose from the couch and went to her desk, grabbing paper, pencil, and a small envelope. "Write your note and then brush your teeth, Jane."

I wasn't sure I trusted Officer D and her police confidentiality anymore. Just in case, I was careful what I wrote.

Hello, Pop!

It's me, your Jane Girl. This Three Boulders place is weird, but I'm staying out of trouble.

I am real good and my hand is fine.

Accidents happen, right, Pop?

Remember what you told me all those years ago?

It's you and me. We got this.

Ten more days, Pop. Get better.

XOXO

Your Jane Girl

I folded the paper, kissed it once, and tucked it into the envelope.

I knew that my note would make Pop's eyeballs get all teary, but he had to remember what he said to me when I was just seven, right before he left for rehab the first time. I remembered everything he had told me, like it was just a second ago.

It all started when I begged and begged him to take me longboarding on Park Street, to teach me to bomb the big hills. Pop was acting weird. His breath smelled yucky, like he hadn't brushed his teeth in days. When we got to the top of the hill, he told me he would demonstrate how it was done, and then he jumped on his board and started cruising down, but he wasn't turning. I started yelling and yelling at him to slow down, to make the zigzags like you do when you longboard. Gravity just took over, and Pop kept going, until . . . until . . . he slammed against a car parked on the side of the road. That thump exploded in my ears, and then my screams exploded. And then I was at the hospital with Pop, and he was in one piece, but it looked like the gazillion tiny stitches over his face and arms and chest were all that held him together. I began to cry because it was my fault Pop was here. I made him take me to Park Street.

That's when he told me about his disease. He said it was like a bad ogre living inside him, but he assured me, *I'm not dying. I just need a little help to get better.*

I said, *I'll help you, Pop. I promise.*

And he said, *You already have. You saved me.* Then he looked right into my eyeballs and he continued, *We ONLY have each other. It's you and me. Jane and Pop. Always. We're two matching socks, Jane Girl. If one of us gets lost, the other one is unmatched and alone. But we got this. We're going to be apart for a bit, but I know where to find you. We can't be kept apart for long. I need you.*

And I said, *I need you too, Pop.*

And that was the honest truth.

And it's still the honest truth.

Day Three

The Three Boulders Vortex

I couldn't find Pop's orange stocking cap the next morning. I looked through the entire black trash bag, but the cap seemed to have vanished. That was Pop's favorite.

"Come on, Jane. You can search later. I need to change your bandage." Officer D was sitting on the couch, unrolling some clean white gauze. In her shirt pocket was my note to Pop, the one she promised not to read.

I peeked one more time under the couch, but I still couldn't see Pop's orange cap. I whisked an old gray stocking cap out of the sack and yanked it over my uncombed hair. I sat down next to Officer D, and she handed me a pain pill and a glass of water. She didn't even ask if I needed one, but her mom-like cop senses were right. I did.

When we got downstairs for breakfast, I heard the hum of voices and the clanking of silverware on plates. I got lots of hellos from the sunshine kids, and offers to sit with them, but I wanted to find G.

She sat in the same spot as yesterday, except today her face was puffy and ghostlier than normal. Even her triangle head seemed kind of flat. I stepped over the bench and sat down.

"G, you look terrible." It was the truth.

"My dad knows what Old Red's big secret is, but he won't tell me. I think it's bad."

Officer D placed a big bowl of oatmeal right in front of me. This was a serious disappointment, worse than whatever bad news Old Red had. Where were the pancakes and bacon and scrambled eggs from yesterday? Mrs. Yarber fed me lumpy oatmeal for the whole twelve days I stayed with that family. It stuck to the top of my mouth. I spit most of it into my napkin when she wasn't looking.

Officer D noticed my scowl. She pushed four smaller bowls toward me, one with brown sugar, another with raisins, another with chopped nuts, and the fourth with chocolate chips. I scooped out sugar and chocolate chips and piled them on top of my oatmeal blob. I took a very small bite.

This Chef Noreen was truly magic. This was like a bowl of mashed cookies, warming my insides.

I heard a raspy throat clearing and turned to see Old Red and Chef Noreen herself standing right behind me.

I had a lump of oatmeal in my mouth, so I didn't say hello, I just gave Chef Noreen a thumbs-up and she smiled a little. She wore a polka-dot sundress with a white apron, and her hair was one thick brown braid, coiled up tight in a hairnet.

"Ernie," Noreen said, looking across the table at Mr. Biggs, "when you see Lester this morning, could you have him find me? I have a shelf in the pantry that is broken."

G leaned into my shoulder, and I think I felt her nerves trickle into my skin, but I just scooped another bite of oatmeal goodness.

"How did that happen?" Mr. Biggs asked.

"I don't know." She pulled off her apron and smoothed her sundress. Her fingers quivered.

"Are you feeling well, Noreen?" Officer D asked.

"Oh," Chef Noreen said, "I'm fine, really. I'm just . . . missing something."

"Ah!" Mr. Biggs said. "Something else vanishing into the Three Boulders vortex."

G laughed at that, but it was a fake laugh. She looked to where Loam and Dandy sat nearby. They were both smiling.

"What's the Three Boulders vortex?" I asked.

"It's the mysterious force that sucks things away," G explained.

"Yes, almost everyone has had something lost in the vortex," Mrs. Biggs added.

"Things just seem to vanish around here," Loam said.

Dandy clapped her hands.

Maybe Pop's orange stocking cap had been sucked into the Three Boulders vortex.

There was a thumping on the floor. It was Old Red, banging his shotgun cane.

"Folks," he rasped. He was pretty loud for an ancient dude. "As you were all told, we have a short church service this morning. Let's meet in the next ten minutes."

"Church?" I looked toward Officer D. "But it's Tuesday. Church is for Sunday."

I was pretty sure that was true, not that me and Pop ever went to church.

"You don't think God accepts prayers on Tuesdays, Jane?" Officer D asked.

Truth was, I didn't know *when* God accepted prayers.

I tried saying prayers lots of times on my own, but God never seemed to answer any of them.

Church

After a second helping of oatmeal, I walked with all the Three Boulders folks to church. We left Noreen's dining hall together and marched like a miniparade across the gravel road and to the fire pit where school had been yesterday. I had been introduced to everyone during my first two days, but it was seriously impossible to remember fifty-six names.

I sat on a log with Officer D on my left and G on my right. Old Red sat in a folding chair watching Mr. Alan Stein and his son toss wood into the flames. The Moonbeam family sat together in a row, crisscross applesauce, right on the dirt with their backs resting against one of the logs. Timmy Spencer and his mom, Amelia, were nearby. Twitchy-body Timmy stood, dropped his hands to the log, and pumped out some push-ups. Chef Noreen was the last person to arrive, her braid still coiled up in the hairnet. Folks were

81

pretty quiet, which is what I expected at church even though I'd never been.

"What are the church laws, G?" I whispered.

She leaned toward me. "Just be a good listener. We start with a song, then a prayer, then a sermon if someone has one, and then community announcements."

"Who's the preacher?"

"There isn't one. Mr. Stein and Mr. Carter give a lot of the sermons because they know some Bible stories. Mr. Moonbeam gave a sermon about birds once, and another time Noreen gave a sermon about making doughnuts."

"What do birds and making doughnuts have to do with God?" I asked, pretty sure she was making this stuff up.

"Everything has to do with God."

I didn't quite know what to say to that, but it didn't matter because Officer D whispered, "Quiet now. Mr. Norton is ready to begin."

Old Red gazed through his thick lenses at all of us perched on the pew logs. He cleared his throat and spoke. "For the sake of time on this Tuesday morning, we will forgo our usual hymns, and begin with a moment of silence or prayer." He lowered his head.

Since I wasn't so sure about praying, I put my head down and thought of Pop. My brain waves sent him good wishes. I silently told him to read my note and say all the right things to those social services folks, so he could come get me and we could get back to Jane-and-Pop good times.

Next Old Red asked, "I know that this service is spur-of-the moment, but does anyone have a sermon prepared?"

There were a few mumbles from the log pews, but no one stepped forward. I was slightly disappointed because hearing about God or birds or doughnuts might be pretty interesting.

"Then I'll get right to my reason for having you all here." Old Red cleared his throat goobers. "I have spoken to every adult now. You know that I am asking each of you to begin making your preparations for leaving Three Boulders."

The air buzzed with loud whispers. G briskly turned toward her parents. I watched them nod to her. Mrs. Biggs's eyes were watery. G shook her frizzy head over and over, like that would make Old Red change his words, make it all just one big joke.

This was the big secret, the answer to all her eavesdropping questions. Everyone *had* to leave boonieville. I put a hand on G's back, but she wouldn't stop shaking her head.

A man sitting between the blondie twins, Megan and Millie, shouted out, "You going to give us an explanation, Red?"

Old Red sucked in a big breath of boonieville air. "I'm an old man, and I believe that part of the reason I have lived to the ripe old age of ninety-one is because so much of my life has been spent on this land, in this little community with all of you and the others who once were a part of Three Boulders."

Mrs. Biggs pulled a tissue out of her pocket and wiped a tear. Chef Noreen squeezed her quivering hands together.

"I may only live another thirty days, or I may live another thirty years."

"Amen!" Mr. Carter shouted out.

"But uncertainty has led me to make a decision. I'm selling this land after all this time. The money will be sufficient for my future health care and living arrangements and leave enough for my other obligations." His eyes scanned every person perched on the log pews, and I swore he gave me an extralong eye gaze.

"Officer Dashell has found an apartment for me in Willis. I plan to move there next month," he said.

"Red"—Mr. Stein rose from his log—"you know some developer will buy this land and turn it into mansions that folks like us could never afford. These firs will be clear-cut and the cabins torn down. That's just not right."

Preston Farmer stood up next and said, "Or someone will turn this place into a hoodlum camp. Those juveniles will destroy our cabins and spray paint the boulders. That isn't right either."

Then Chef Noreen slowly rose. She finally pulled off that hairnet and her thick braid flopped down her back. Her hands still quivered. "Or," she began, "nothing will be done with the land, and our little homes and garden and fire pit and the community we love will simply disintegrate. And that's the worst possibility of all."

Folks grumbled in agreement, and teardrops rolled down cheeks. Finally Old Red raised his arm, requesting silence.

"I agree that those are all possibilities, but I just can't worry about that anymore. I need the money, now more than ever."

"Are you in trouble, Red?" Mr. Moonbeam hollered out.

Old Red turned to the man and said, "No. It's not *me* who's in trouble. It's someone I care about deeply."

And right after he said those words, there was a gust of wind. My loose hairs swept across my nostrils, tickling me.

I couldn't help but wonder if that wind was God talking to all of us. I figured God probably needed his own special way to communicate, since I didn't think there were cell towers or satellites up in heaven. God must have had a reason for sending that windy message right at that moment, just when Old Red said someone was in trouble. I looked at every person resting on those log pews, wondering if that person in trouble was sitting here in this nature church. G was listening to God's message too. Her eyeballs were scanning the crowd just like mine, but hers were drippy with tears.

"Well, folks, I know this is tough news," Officer D said, her cop face tight and stern, "but some of us need to be getting off to town for the day." She lifted her hefty body off the log pew, her whacking stick slapping her thigh. "I suggest you chat with Red privately about your concerns."

Officer D gave me a pat on the shoulder, and she turned and headed back to the main gravel road with a few other adults behind her.

And so I sat there in the Three Boulders church with my aching hand and wrist, surrounded by God and a bunch of upset boonievillers, and I reminded myself that all this news about the end of Three Boulders was no concern of mine. My main concern was still the same—getting through these next ten days.

And right then, G shot off the log pew and ran.

The Three Boulders

That Gertrude Biggs could move for a girl in a skirt, lugging a backpack full of journals.

I tucked my bandaged hand against my belly and ran behind her, up the church path to the main gravel road. I passed the softball field, where a couple deer were grazing in the outfield, and the empty dining hall. I ran up the road that was hugged by all the tiny log cabins, but then I lost G. She had vanished into the trees ahead. I slowed to a walk, not sure where I was going anymore. I hadn't been beyond the road yet.

I was on a narrow path that wound through giant clumps of trees. The path had squishy pine needles that cushioned my feet better than that gravel. It was shady and cool inside all these tall trees and bushes, but ahead I could see sunlight.

When I reached that sunlight, most of the trees

disappeared. I stood in a grassy clearing and ahead of me were three of the most enormous rocks I had ever seen.

They were clumped together: one in the back, like a tall arched tower; the second, low and flat to the ground; and the third, fat and round, just to the right of the flat rock. The sun beat down on them and they sparkled like glitter. I thought I could see little rays of magical electric stuff come off them. If I touched one of them, maybe I'd absorb some strange power. Maybe it was God's power. A tingle rippled through my whole body. I wished Pop could see these rocks.

G sat on the flat rock. She had her knees drawn up under her chin, hugging them tight. I sat down next to her and touched the hard gray surface.

G had a glazy, spaced-out look on her face. I couldn't tell what she was feeling. Maybe these boulders put a spell on her, a calmness spell. The really weird thing was that maybe I was feeling that same spell.

"Are these *the* three boulders?"

"Yes." G lowered her knees, stretching her legs forward. She smoothed her long skirt over her thighs. "The tall, spiked one is called Redemption. This big round one is called Forgiveness." She patted the round rock. "The one we are sitting on is called Community."

"Someone named them?"

"Old Red did," G answered. "Mountains and rivers have names, why not boulders?"

Redemption? Community? Forgiveness?

"But those are *terrible* names," I said. "That's like calling a dog Happiness or a tree Beauty. These rocks deserve great names."

I jumped off the flat rock and stepped a few paces backward so I could view all three boulders.

"The tall one is definitely the coolest, and it rules over the others. It should be named something like . . . Majestic Arch."

G turned her neck and peered up at the spiky boulder.

"And the flat one reminds me of a turtle's shell. It should be something like Tortoise Back. And the round one"—I paused—"well, it looks like steel. Maybe it could be . . . Steel Marble."

"The names are symbols," G said.

That was plain crazy, if you asked me. I jumped back onto the flat boulder and sat down again.

"I think things should just be what they are," I said. "In fourth grade, my teacher read this poem about a flower, and she said it was filled with stuff that the flower symbolized and that the poem was a beautiful statement of love. That made no sense to me. If the poet wanted to tell me about love, why didn't he just say it?"

G pulled her knees up to her chest again. She kind of laughed and said, "The names represent what Three Boulders is all about."

Redemption. Forgiveness. Community. My brain wasn't ready to think too hard about those names. I thought they were dumb, no matter what they represented.

G got quiet again. I noticed her blue journal resting next to her, the People of Three Boulders.

"Are you writing in your journals?"

She shook her head. "I'm just looking at all the people who live here and wondering where they will go."

"I'm sorry you have to leave, G. Maybe you can move to Willis. It's an okay town. Pop and me have lived there for almost a year. There's real town-like things there. You know, McDonald's, grocery stores, paved roads, parks. All the stuff you don't have here."

"But I like it here. It's my home. I don't need all those town-like things." She had teardrops in the corners of her eyes. "Don't you have someplace that's truly your home?"

"Of course. I have Pop. My home is wherever Pop is."

I could tell by the way G tilted her frizzy head that she was trying to understand what I was saying. G was a thinker.

"The only thing that matters is that I'm with Pop. We're a matching pair of socks, me and Pop. We fold up together perfectly."

"Then why did Officer D bring you to Three Boulders without him?" G asked.

I was surprised by her question because it didn't sound

like the polite, law-abiding, journal-toting Gertrude Biggs I met two days ago.

"If I tell you, are you going to write it down in those journals?"

"Not if you don't want me to."

And I believed her because her brown eyeballs stared directly at my gray eyeballs.

"I'm here because Pop is sick."

"Oh, I'm sorry." G put her hand on my back. "Is it . . . is it cancer?"

I jerked, which knocked her hand away. "No!" I said, probably louder than necessary. "He doesn't have cancer! He's just in the hospital in Willis for a while. Twelve days, actually."

"Why?"

I wasn't sure the best way to explain to G about Pop and the bad ogre inside him. I wasn't completely sure that she would understand. Not many people did, not my teachers, not the foster people I had to stay with, and definitely not the nosy social services people. No one understood Pop like I did. "He's in rehab," I said. "Because of his drinking too much."

G gazed at me. I think she had to take a moment to find that word in her brain dictionary.

"He'll be fine," I hurried to explain." He always gets

better in rehab. Twelve days, and he's dry as a camel's mouth in the desert. That's what he always tells me."

"*Always?* You mean he's been in rehab before?"

She looked at me again as though Pop was dying, so I explained. "Just 'cause he drinks a little doesn't make him a bad pop. He's sad sometimes, that's all, and when he gets sad, he drinks, and then he just needs some medicine. That's why he goes to rehab. It's like medicine to make him feel better." I started rubbing my wrist. Thinking of Pop's sadness and his drinking made it ache a whole lot. I tried to think of some good me-and-Pop times instead, like when he taught me to make a grilled cheese sandwich, and when he showed me how to use the right tools to fix the broken porch steps.

G watched me rub my wrist. "What happened to your hand?"

I stopped rubbing and swallowed a gulp of air. My brain swirled with a memory, a memory that was *not* a good me-and-Pop time. "I burned it."

And that was mostly the honest truth.

"Oh. Did—"

"My pop is a good pop," I added quickly.

G put her hands behind her, propping herself on the flat surface of Tortoise Back. "I'm glad," she said. "I'm glad he's a good pop to you." Her fingers stroked the hard rock. "Three

Boulders is a good home to me."

Then we were just quiet, sitting there on those stu-
pidly named boulders, staring at the clump of pine trees
in the distance, thinking our sad and happy thoughts, side
by side.

Day Four

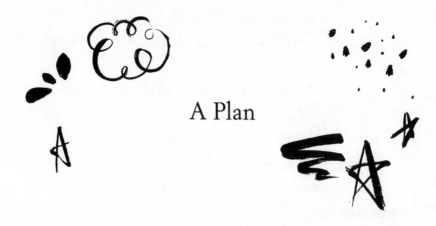

A Plan

On Wednesday, my fourth day in Three Boulders, G informed me that once a week, all the kids spend two hours working in the community garden. This was yet another weird law of Three Boulders, and I was pretty sure I wasn't going to like it too much.

As we walked through the garden gate, I breathed in the smell of cow poop, and I plugged my nose. But I also took my first good look at everything. This garden was beautiful enough to be pictured in fancy magazines. These folks took care of their plants. G said that the wooden rectangle sections were raised beds, and I followed her along the pebble paths that wove through the beds.

We joined the other kids at the shed where Mr. Biggs stood, passing out tools and gloves.

"Jane!" he said. "You have your yellow shirt. That makes you an official Three Boulders student."

"Just for nine more days. That's all."

"Might as well be nine days for all of us," pudgy Mitchell Landau complained.

"Chin up, Mitchell," Mr. Biggs said firmly. "Chins up, everyone. We need to be more accepting of all this. Mr. Norton wouldn't sell this land if it wasn't necessary."

The sunshine kids stood still, staring at Mr. Biggs.

"Tonight we are having a special record night. Mr. Norton thought Jane might like to see one while she's here." He smiled at me, then turned to the short girl standing next to Marty, "Lizzie, are you ready to continue the challenge to be Three Boulders' top speller?"

"Yes!"

G whispered to me, "Lizzie and Mrs. Carter are having an ongoing spelling bee. Neither one has missed a word in the last four months. Lizzie is only nine."

Mr. Biggs continued. "We haven't had a speed multiplication challenge for quite some time, so we'll do that tonight. All of you will be in that challenge."

"Speed multiplication?" I said.

That's a dumb record.

"Yes, Jane. Five minutes. Five pages of multiplication problems. We'll see who gets the most completed and correct. Our current record holder is Mr. Stein. Loam, you were so close to beating him last month."

Dandy clapped her hands.

"Anyone who wants some speed practice can come to my cabin today." He picked up a shovel and handed it to Loam. "All right, everyone have gloves? Gertie, please help Jane."

G looked at my hand with the fresh bandages Officer D had changed earlier, then pulled out some plastic gloves. "Here, put this on your burned hand so it doesn't get dirty. Maybe only use your right hand to pull weeds."

Mr. Biggs made one final announcement. "Okay, work hard, kids, and let's meet at the fire pit after lunch to discuss our nature projects." He left the garden as G stretched the plastic glove over my bandage.

Blondie Millie Donald searched in the shed, scratching her head. "The Three Boulders vortex has sucked away my favorite purple gloves."

"I haven't been able to find that little silver trowel for weeks," Marty Landau said.

"What difference does it make?" twin blondie Megan added. "We're all leaving. I don't know why we're bothering in this garden."

"Because we aren't leaving today," G said. "It's Wednesday and we work in the garden on Wednesday." She handed me a short digging tool and led me to a bed with a sign that said Turnips. She leaned over her long tool and began poking in the dirt.

"How come we're working in the turnip section?" I asked. "Nobody actually eats turnips."

"You did last night," G said. "They were in the beef stew."

Oh. Last night's stew was nothing but spicy meat and veggie deliciousness.

"Well, still. Can we work in the tomato section? I like tomatoes."

G shook her head. "No. This is my family's crop. Preston Farmer assigned us turnips, so that's what we tend."

"Who has the tomatoes?"

"The Steins."

"What veggie does Officer D have?"

"She doesn't have one. She's busy during the weekdays, so Mr. Farmer has her help with turning the compost on Saturdays or Sundays."

This Preston Farmer was a good organizer, but I hoped there would be no compost turning for me while I was here. That sounded smelly.

"Hey, Gertie, I can help you today," Loam said. "My mom was so upset yesterday about Mr. Norton's announcement that she came down to the garden and pulled every weed she saw in the spinach bed."

Dandy, standing close to her brother, clapped her hands.

"My dad's been angry for three days now, ever since he learned the news. He doesn't want to move back to a city," the Stein kid said. I couldn't remember his first name.

Timmy Spencer added, "Mama spent the whole day

with Miss Noreen in the kitchen. She said they cried tears into the stew last night."

"Daddy said that Sunday will be our last softball game," Lizzie Cooper added. "I just learned to bunt."

I leaned over and pulled a little weed from the turnip bed, listening to the sunshine kids complain. No one was doing much work.

The blondie twins moved toward Dandy and had a group hug. "We're going to miss seeing you each day, Dandy." And they squeezed that poor weed girl, holding down her flappy hands.

"This is so unfair of Mr. Norton." The Stein kid spoke again, which started the eyeball waterworks, at least from the blondies and Lizzie Cooper and even G.

I was tired of all this whining, so I dropped my little digger and said, "Remember what Mr. Biggs said? He said 'chins up.'" I looked at them all. Their shirts didn't seem so sunny with their sad faces. "If none of your families want to leave this place, why don't you do something about it?"

"What can we do, Jane?" Millie asked. "Mr. Norton made his decision. It's his land."

"But he's going to *sell* the land," I said. "You all seem to think this boonie place with your record nights and fire pit church is pretty great. If you all want to stay so badly, why don't all your families just *buy* the land from Mr. Norton?"

Those nine sunshine kids got dead silent. I might have

been able to hear their brains ticking together like one big machine if I listened close enough.

"Of course!" G said. "Jane, that's so simple, but it's brilliant!"

There was a big smile on my inside right then. People *never* said I was brilliant.

I reached into my cargo shorts pocket and pulled out three quarters. "Here." I put my hand toward G. "You can have these. I have more money in Officer D's room in my sack."

G smiled at me and then she took command. "Okay. This is what we'll do. Everyone talk with your parents tonight. Ask them about their money situation. We'll meet tomorrow morning before breakfast down at the church fire pit."

"Before breakfast?" Loam asked.

"Of course. This is important. This plan could save Three Boulders!" G said.

Dandy Moonbeam began clapping, which got all the other sunshine club kids clapping too.

This was a good plan.

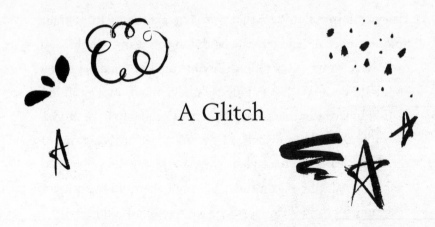

A Glitch

I took that plan seriously too. I dug in my plastic sack later that afternoon as I waited for Officer D to get back from Willis. I found six one-dollar bills, seven quarters, five dimes, ten nickels, and 28 pennies. I used my excellent adding skills and calculated that I had $9.03. I tucked two dollars back into the pocket of one of my hoodies for emergencies, and set the rest on the little table next to my lumpy couch bed.

The door opened and Officer D entered the room wearing her serious cop face. I figured she'd had a rough day down in Willis. Probably had to arrest all kinds of bad guys. My plan to buy Three Boulders would cheer her up for sure. I knew how much she loved this place. Maybe as much as G.

"Officer D, look!" I jumped off the couch and pointed at my money on the table. "All the Three Boulders kids are collecting money. I figured since people were sad about leaving Three Boulders that everyone should just put their money together and *buy* the land. Do you want to help? Do you have some extra money in your pockets or maybe in a bank down in Willis? Pop doesn't have much money in the bank, but you have a good job, so you probably have more."

I couldn't help myself. My words were spewing out of control. Officer D raised her man paw, giving me her special silent signal. She sat on the couch, but she didn't comment on money or my idea. Her cop face remained unbroken.

"Let's talk." She patted the couch, and I sat next to her. She put her hand on my knee. "Jane, there's been a glitch with your pop."

I knew about glitches. Glitches were nothing but annoyances, stuff that slowed you down, like planning to make a grilled cheese sandwich and then finding the outside of the cheese has a layer of mold and you have to slice off all the furriness before you can begin making the sandwich. That was a glitch.

I didn't like glitches.

Ever.

"What are you talking about? Did he break a rule in rehab? Did he miss a meeting? What kind of glitch?" Question marks shot off their dots like bullets in my brain.

Pop never had glitches during rehab. He was a perfect twelve-day patient. In and out. Done. All better. Back to *good* Jane-and-Pop times.

Officer D shook her head firmly. She glanced at my hand. "No, Jane. His rehab is going fine."

"Then what is it?"

She looked up at the ceiling before she spoke, like there were words stored up there that needed to drop into her head. "Today, your pop was interviewed by social services."

Social services *again*. Those interfering people and their questions that made my belly twist like Slinky coils.

"So?" I prodded her.

Now she looked at me with her worried face, and that worried *me*.

A lot.

"Jane, I brought Fran from social services back to Three Boulders with me. She wants to talk to you again." Officer D moved to the door and pushed it open.

Social services Fran stepped into the room. She was the person assigned to me and Pop. She was the one who placed me with Mrs. Dubois when we moved to Willis. She was the one who visited me and Pop every month and checked out our house. She was the one who talked to me Saturday night in the hospital. I stood up and glared at her.

"Hello, Jane." She moved toward the couch.

I moved away from the couch.

"You don't need to be afraid. I just want to ask you some more questions."

"I'm not afraid," I said.

Not even close to the honest truth.

Officer D stood behind me and put both hands on my shoulders, clamping down hard, but not a mean clamp down. I didn't want her to let go.

"Would you like to sit down?" Fran asked.

I shook my head. I was going to talk as little as humanly possible.

"I spoke with your father today."

I sealed my lips tight.

"I asked him about the night your hand was burned."

I was stone silent. I looked at her shoes. They were shiny orange red, like fire.

"His story is different from the story you told me when you were in the hospital." She peered at my hand.

"What did he say?" I asked, breaking my silence.

"I can't tell you, Jane. Just like I can't tell him the story *you* shared."

My chest loaded up with worry. What could Pop have said?

Flame-shoed Fran pulled some papers out of her purse. "These are notes from your initial interview, after the incident."

I leaned again into Officer D's chest and she squeezed my shoulders tighter.

Flame-shoed Fran sat down on the lumpy couch. "Jane,

is there any information you perhaps forgot to tell us about that night?"

I shook my head again. I didn't *forget* anything.

"Is there anything else you can *add* to your story?"

Another head shake.

"What was your father doing when your hand and wrist were burned?" Fran asked.

"I already told you that. It's in your notes."

Officer D gripped my shoulders tighter. "Jane, just answer the question. This is important to your case."

My twitchy brain syndrome shifted into high power. Brain cells were whirling around faster and faster. I wanted social services Fran to go away. "He . . ." Now my fingers were starting to twitch. "He was resting a bit—"

"He was resting?" Fran interrupted me. "You didn't mention that earlier." She pulled out a pen and jotted some notes.

I gulped. Crud and a half!

"Well, I didn't mention it because . . ."

Think. Think. Think.

"Because it wasn't anything weird. Pop works hard at the warehouse. He rests on the couch every night." I inhaled and kept going, remembering the story I told in the hospital. "So I went into the kitchen, and I turned on Pop's music that we like to dance to when we make dinner."

This was mostly the honest truth. Me and Pop did dance to music. Some nights.

"And Pop joined me when he was all done resting." I turned my head and looked up at Officer D still behind me. She gazed back with her worried face.

"And then it happened just like I said before. I slipped and fell, and my hand landed on the stove, and it really hurt bad. Pop called nine-one-one right away, and then the cops and the medical guys came, and then I was in the hospital with Officer D and you. That's what happened." I rattled that story off my tongue fast and furious, and I wasn't going to say anything else about it.

Flame-shoed Fran scribbled all over the notes in her lap. Then she put her pen down and exhaled slowly. "Jane, there's a bit of a problem here. With two different stories from you and your father, I may need more time to sort this all out. You may not be able to return to your father as anticipated."

My heart slammed against my ribs, almost hard enough to stop it from beating. What needed to be sorted out? What had Pop said?

"How *much* more time?" My hand and wrist pulsed with pain.

Officer D let go of my shoulders and turned me to face her. "We don't know, Jane," she said.

This wasn't good. I swallowed a gulp of air because I felt tears coming into my eyes, but I couldn't cry. If I started crying, I might let everything out, everything about what really happened that night. I couldn't do that.

"Jane, are you sure you don't want to tell us anything else?" Officer D asked. Her worry-parent-like face was begging me.

"No," I answered quickly, too quickly maybe. "Can she leave now?"

Officer D and flame-shoed Fran exchanged looks. Fran returned the papers to her purse and rose from the couch, not saying anything else.

"I'm going to walk Fran down the path to her car, Jane," Officer D said. "I'll be back. We'll go to dinner and record night together."

There was no way I was going to record night. My brain had too much sorting to do. What record could I possibly break in this boonieville anyway? Kid with the most foster homes?

I flung Officer D's soft brown blanket around my back and curled up on the couch. I thought I had everything in order. I was picking Pop up, like he picked me up. That was what we did. But now everything was going wrong. Now I had to do something to fix all this, something to get me back to Pop at the end of our twelve days. I had to *see* Pop and talk to him. I had to tell him what to say, so his story matched mine. If they matched, we'd be back together. Another successful twelve days. I was sure of that.

There was just one problem. They don't allow visitors in rehab centers. They don't even allow phone calls or emails.

I knew if I could just *get* to Willis, I would figure out how to see Pop.

But I needed to do it soon.

I only had eight days.

Day Five

Teaming Up

I must have had lots of bad thoughts swirling in my head because I dreamed of Misha that night. Misha, my sweet, soft bunny that me and Pop adopted from the animal shelter. She lived in our living room in a wooden, two-room hutch that Pop built. When we watched TV in the evenings, Misha would sometimes hop back and forth on our laps, and we would give her little pieces of apple. Me and Pop loved her lots. She was our third sock, a trio. Me and Pop and Misha. She made our family bigger, and I loved that a lot. I even wondered if maybe our family could grow more. Me and Pop and Misha and . . . maybe . . . but I knew I shouldn't think thoughts like that. I had Pop. Pop had me. We both had Misha.

But then one day we didn't.

We were having some bad me-and-Pop days. One night, when I went to bed, Pop told me he would put Misha back in her hutch, but he didn't. When I got up the next morning, Pop was still crashed on the couch, and Misha wasn't in her hutch. The door was wide open. I wandered all over our house, calling her name, looking in little hidey-holes where a bunny might snuggle in. Finally, I found her under Pop's bed, lying stiff, a chewed electrical cord near her nose.

I opened my eyes and jerked upright on the couch.

I had a woozy, dizzy feeling inside me. It was probably from my Misha dream, or it could have been from worrying so much about social services Fran and about Pop *and* how I was going to be able to talk to him.

That wooziness continued as Officer D bandaged up my hand.

"You're quiet this morning, Jane." She turned my wrist, and I tensed up my belly tight.

"Just thinking about stuff, that's all," I said. "I need to be at the fire pit before breakfast."

Officer D didn't say anything else, and when she finished my hand, I pulled the same gray hoodie that I wore yesterday over my head and walked downstairs.

The morning air was crisp in this boonieville, and I sucked in a deep breath. It helped take away some of my morning dizziness. I was pretty sure Pop would tell me that the fresh piney scent was good for my lungs. Pop was a big lover of fresh air.

G was perched on a pew log at the fire pit with six other kids.

"Hi, Jane," they all said together.

"Where were you last night? You missed record night," Millie asked.

I kicked at one of the logs. "I wasn't feeling too good." Honest truth.

"Now we're just waiting on Loam and Dandy," G said, tapping her pencil. She had a notebook open on her lap with three columns drawn.

"Maybe Loam forgot," Timmy Spencer said. He was doing more push-ups. Today his toes were propped on the log and his hands were on the dirt.

"He's probably still asleep," Mitchell Landau suggested.

G sighed and put her notebook on the log. "Jane and I will go find him. You guys can all begin filling out this chart with how much money your families can pitch in. We'll be right back."

I was happy to be alone with G for a bit. It gave me time for my questions.

"Hey, G, besides Officer D, who else goes into Willis each day?" I began.

"Why do you want to know?"

"I'm just curious about this Three Boulders place and how it works."

That was one lame lie. G peered at me for a long spell as we shuffled along the path.

"A lot of people work in Willis: Loam's dad, Branch Moonbeam; Preston Farmer; Amelia Spencer; Alan Stein—"

"Do they all drive their cars into town?" I interrupted.

"Some do, but some of them ride together. They use Old Red's van."

My brain had to sort that through. Could I stow away in the back of the van and get to Willis?

"That's real smart of them to ride together." I did my best to sound casually interested. "What time do they leave in the morning?"

G shot me another glance, and I could feel the rays of suspicion firing out of her eyeballs. "They leave pretty early most days, around six thirty."

That wouldn't work. Officer D would be suspicious if I got up that early. I kicked up a spray of pine needles.

There had to be a different way.

"Didn't you tell me that some folks go into town to do shopping and get supplies and stuff?"

G shifted her backpack onto her other shoulder. "Yes, my mom helps with that on Wednesdays."

Wednesday was yesterday.

Double crud.

This was such a crazy place with its laws and schedules.

What if a person needed something on a Thursday or a Friday?

Going to Willis was crammed-to-the-top full of trouble, but I *had* to talk to Pop. I had to know what Pop told social services Fran. We had to get our stories straight.

It was time for the honest truth. If there was one person I could trust in this place it was G.

"Will you help me get to Willis, G?" I asked, my eyeballs pleading. "I have to talk to my pop."

G fidgeted with her backpack straps. "Can't you just ask Officer Dashell?"

"No. Nobody can know. I'm not allowed to see Pop when he's in rehab. They *never* let me. Each time he goes they have to do an investigation. They ask us both questions. They make sure everything is okay between me and Pop—"

"Is everything okay?" She was staring at my burned hand.

"Of course." I tucked my hand in my hoodie pocket. I'm not sure G believed me, even though it was mostly the truth.

"You could get in serious trouble."

I nodded again. Believe me, I knew.

Stay out of trouble, Jane Girl. Trouble might keep us apart longer.

G stopped in the middle of the gravel road. She looked up at all the clouds in the boonieville sky. "Do you know what happens to folks who break too many of the laws in Three Boulders?"

I shook my head.

"They get told to leave," G said. She picked up a handful of pebbles in the road.

"I don't really live here, G. I'm only visiting, remember?"

"And I will only live here for a little while longer." She bounced the pebbles in her palm a few moments. Then she stepped forward and hurled her pebbles up the road. Hard. Almost tripping on her long skirt.

"Okay." She turned back toward me. "We'll figure out a way to get to Willis so you can see your pop, and I'll come with you."

I wanted to kiss G. But I don't do kissing.

G picked up another handful of pebbles, and I grabbed some too.

Side by side, we chucked our rocks high into the Three Boulders sky. They clinked together in the air, dropping to the ground as one team.

Me and G high-fived.

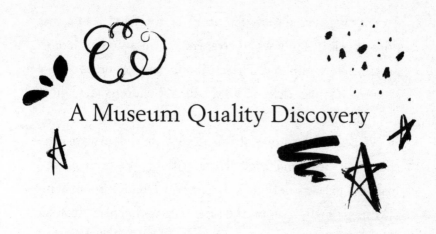

A Museum Quality Discovery

"Let's get Loam and Dandy and finish our Three Boulders business before we work on the Willis plans," G suggested as we continued up cabin row.

That sounded A-OK with me. Just knowing G was going to help me was like finding a piece of candy in my pocket, a super-sweet surprise.

"Here's the Moonbeams' cabin." G pointed to the one with all the birdhouses nailed onto the porch railings.

She knocked on the door, and we waited. There was no answer. She knocked harder. Still no answer.

"Let's just go in," I suggested. "Maybe they're still asleep."

I half expected G to be shocked at that suggestion, but she shrugged and turned the doorknob.

"Hello?" she called. No one answered.

The inside of the Moonbeams' cabin looked like G's

except there wasn't any furniture in the front room, just piles of colorful pillows all arranged on the wooden floor in an arc, like a rainbow. These Moonbeams sat on the floor at home just like they sat on the dirt at church. They must not like chairs.

G peeked into one of the three inside doorways. She shook her head and tried the next door. We both peered inside. This was definitely Loam and Dandy's room with two single mattresses on the floor, one with a black blanket and the other with a pink blanket. "They aren't here," G said. "Maybe Loam forgot and went to the dining hall."

I was about to follow her when something caught my eye. The closet door was slightly open and something orange was on the floor. It looked like Pop's stocking cap, the one that was missing. I moved to the closet and picked it up. It *was* Pop's cap.

How did it get here?

And then I opened the closet door the whole way, and what I saw may not have solved the mysteries of the universe, but it did solve one of the mysteries of boonieville Three Boulders.

"Uh . . . G? Come here. You gotta see this."

If it was humanly possible to make G's frizzy hair go straight, seeing the inside of Loam and Dandy's closet did the trick. She grew ten inches taller just staring into that closet. No words came out of her mouth.

120

"It's the Three Boulders vortex," I said. "Now you know where everything went."

But this was not just a closet crammed full of missing items. This was different. This had taken some true dedication, and it was . . . beautiful.

Seriously beautiful.

Because inside the closet was a tall bookcase, and on every shelf the contraband was stacked and layered by color in perfect rainbow order. Red items on the top shelf. Then orange. Then yellow, and so on. If there was a world-famous rainbow museum, this bookshelf belonged there.

But G didn't see it that way. "He's a thief! Look, Jane! There are Millie's purple gloves. There's Mr. Carter's baseball cap. Those blue hair bands belong to Mrs. Spencer. Oh, there's an old People of Three Boulders journal!" She scanned every single shelf. "Jane! There's that bottle of alcohol. He never—"

G couldn't finish her thought, though, because in the doorway, elbow to elbow, appeared Loam and Dandy.

"What are you doing in our cabin?" Loam exclaimed.

G didn't answer that question. She laid into Loam. "You stole all these things!"

Loam stepped forward, reaching out to touch G's arm. "Gertie, I can explain."

But G moved backward toward me. "How do you explain being a thief, Loam? You've stolen something from every person in Three Boulders and then blamed it on some nonexistent vortex."

Dandy reached into the back pocket of Loam's jeans and pulled out a pale yellow handkerchief. She flapped it in the air a few times and stood in front of the rainbow masterpiece, eyeballing the shelves. She wadded the handkerchief and placed it on the yellow shelf between a little rubber ducky and a candle, precisely filling in a small gap. Then she spun two circles and clapped her hands.

"Dandy," Loam said, "go find Mom in the dining hall. I need to talk to Gertie and Jane."

Dandy pulled on her brother's arm.

"Go. I'll be there soon." He hugged her. She clapped her hands again and left the little cabin.

I wasn't sure if G was going to hurl or if she was going to lunge into Loam like an attack dog. She looked a little foamy around the mouth.

Loam plopped down on his mattress. "Dandy made that. The whole arrangement." He pointed at the closet. "She's been working on it for two years, ever since we came to Three Boulders."

"But *you* took all those things, didn't you?" G asked.

Loam nodded. His eyelids were saggy. "It's kind of a long story."

I sat down on Dandy's mattress, ready to listen. I was getting that dizzy feeling inside again, like I had when I woke up from my bad-memory dream. G remained standing, her arms crossed. "I want the short version, Loam."

"Before we moved here, we lived in Eugene. One day, we were in the Seven-Eleven, and I watched Dandy take this pack of gum off the shelf. She shoved it in her pocket. I knew I should have said something, but I didn't because . . . because, you know, she's Dandy, and she doesn't—" He shrugged.

I knew exactly what he meant.

"I asked Dandy about it when we got home and that's when she showed me her rainbow. It was under her bed in a long box she'd found in the garage. It was filled with colored items she had taken from our house, our friends' houses, and even stores. I think her head works different, and when she sees something that she knows will fit into one of her rainbow holes, she has to have it."

"Wait. Are you saying *Dandy* took all that stuff in the closet?" I asked.

Loam shook his head. "No, it was me. I started taking stuff for Dandy because I didn't want her to get in trouble. Mom and Dad were worrying about her a lot. I wanted to help her. Her rainbows made her happy. She's good at it."

My eyeballs glanced again into the closet. Loam was right. Dandy was great at rainbows.

"But that's wrong. No matter how pretty it looks or how much Dandy likes to make rainbows, you can't steal stuff for her," G said, but she didn't sound quite so mad anymore, and she lowered herself down next to me on the mattress.

"I know," he said. "I got caught on the security camera one day, pocketing two bottles of nail polish that Dandy wanted. They called our parents, and I had to confess everything. They were shocked about what Dandy and I were doing. They thought we needed a new environment, one without the temptation of stores and shoplifting." Loam paused. He was rubbing his hands together. "My dad knew the Coopers from way back, and the Coopers talked to Mr. Norton, and he let us all come live here."

"But you kept stealing," G said.

"I didn't at first," he said. "But Dandy and I shared this room, and she started making her rainbows with her own stuff, and then one day, we were in the dining hall and she was staring at this blue coffee cup, clapping her hands."

"So you took the cup?" I said.

He nodded. "And then I took other stuff for her, and then her rainbow got bigger and bigger, and she moved it all to the bookshelf in our closet, and now I just can't seem to stop."

I knew right then that Loam had a bad ogre inside him like Pop, and I knew just how hard it was to keep that ogre away. Pop would fight his ogre for weeks and months, sometimes longer, but that ogre was mean and strong, and he kept coming back.

"Loam," G said, "people are missing all that stuff. I don't understand."

He sniffed and wiped the sleeve of his shirt across his nose. "I'm sorry, Gertie. I really am. I know you can't understand."

But I did. I understood completely. Loam and Dandy were matching socks.

Sometimes you just had to do things for someone you loved, even if it might get you in trouble, even if you knew that other people wouldn't understand.

Sometimes you just had to.

"Gertie, please don't tell anyone. *Please*," Loam begged.

"I don't know if I can keep this a secret. I'm the town record keeper. And besides, with everyone leaving soon, you're going to get caught."

"I'm begging you, Gertie." He folded his hands together, like he was praying. "I'm your friend. Please keep it a secret for just a while until I figure out what to do."

"I'll keep it a secret," I said. "But me and G need your help with something."

My brain amazed me at times because right at that very moment, even though I was sitting in Loam and Dandy's rainbow vortex of stolen stuff, I managed to think of a plan to get into Willis and see Pop.

Dirt boy was going to join our team.

This plan was going to be foolproof.

Day Six

On Our Way

I woke up early the next morning, but it wasn't because of bad me-and-Pop dreams, or because I was worried about our Willis plan.

I woke up early because my hand was throbbing worse than ever. I gazed at it in the dim morning light and gently peeled back the tape and gauze. Yucky goobers blobbed up on some of the red marks. I ran my pointy finger along my skin and cringed, squeezing in the cries of pain that wanted out real bad.

Officer D was still sleeping. That was good. I couldn't let her see my burn She'd get her worry face on and probably take me to a doctor which would ruin all my plans for getting to Pop. I had to handle this.

On the table next to my couch was fresh gauze and the white goopy stuff Officer D had been using each day. I managed to squeeze some of the goop into my good hand

and I rubbed it on, slowly, 'cause it stung worse than a fuming wasp each time I touched those burns. Then I unwound the clean gauze and spiraled it around my hand and wrist, taping it down as best I could.

By the time Officer D woke, I was dressed and sitting on the couch organizing my plans and worries inside my brain.

"Officer D, look what I did." I held up my arm so she could see my handiwork.

"You taped it up yourself, Jane?"

I nodded, trying to smile and hide all the serious, throbby achiness I was still feeling.

Officer D inspected my first aid. "Not bad. Did you remember the cream?" She lifted a corner of the tape and readjusted it. I pulled back my arm just a bit so she wouldn't unwrap it all.

"Yes. I did it just like you. I thought it was time for me to start doing it myself. Pop always says that's important—doing stuff yourself, I mean."

"I agree. Building independence is important," she said. "How's the pain this morning?"

Now it was time to lie. "Oh, not bad, but maybe one of those pills would be good."

Officer D went to get my medicine. I breathed out a tiny sigh of relief that she didn't question me more.

She dropped the pill into my good hand and set a glass

of water on the side table. "Jane, I'm heading into Willis early this morning to visit a few folks, so I won't have breakfast with you today. You can sit with Gertie's family again." She lifted my chin like she had before and gave me a little smile. For a moment, I felt a fuzziness inside me.

"Okay," I said because this was good news. Having Officer D out of my way this morning could be perfect—as long as Loam stuck with our plan.

Just a bit later, I headed downstairs to the dining hall for some breakfast. Maybe some of Chef Noreen's grub would make my burn feel better.

Not a lot of folks had arrived for breakfast yet, but Loam was sitting with G at the end of one of the long picnic tables, just like we had discussed yesterday. His hair was a disaster. His eyes were sleepy.

I stepped over the bench and parked myself right next to him. "Any changes?" I said, grabbing a slice of bacon.

"No," Loam said. "My dad is leaving at his normal time, eight o'clock."

"Do you have the key?" I whispered.

"It's already in your pocket."

And sure enough, like the slick, secretive klepto he was, he had managed to slide that car key into my hoodie pocket without me even noticing.

He was *good*. No wonder he hadn't been caught.

"And the blanket? It's in the car?"

He nodded. G nodded too.

"And your dad said you could go with him to Willis? He's not suspicious?" I crunched another bite of bacon.

"He's cool," Loam said. "He lets me go into work with him once a month."

"And, G?" I said. "You talked to your pop?"

"Yes. He thinks that you and I are spending the day working on our nature project."

I knew that lying to Mr. Biggs was hard for G. I wasn't going to let her down by getting caught. Our plan was foolproof.

I guzzled some orange juice and chomped one more piece of bacon. I looked up at the clock on the dining hall wall.

7:35. We had to move.

Me and G slipped out the front door and jogged down the crooked path. The twigs from the low bushes scratched at our legs. My wrist was screaming loud, but I kept going. G ran ahead of me, her backpack bouncing on her shoulders.

When we got to the grassy parking lot at the end of the path, just a few cars were left. Officer D's banged-up truck was gone, which was a big relief. I slipped the key into the lock of the old silver boat car and opened the doors. Me and G climbed into the back seat, locking all the doors before we crouched down on the floor of the car. The long bench seat in the front was perfect for hiding us.

For a nanosecond my hand didn't ache at all 'cause having G with me made me feel better. She'd been my company since I arrived in crazy Three Boulders. Actually, I think she'd been my friend, and I'd never had too many of those.

I spread the blanket Loam had left for me in the back seat so it covered both of us. We were tucked in little balls, thighs against our chests, chins between our knees. I thought this would be a good time to practice my new silent praying skills, the ones I learned in Three Boulders church. I prayed that we wouldn't get caught, and I prayed that I would be able to see Pop, and I prayed that my hand would get better.

The driver's door opened. I felt the car dip to the left as Mr. Moonbeam climbed inside, giving the door a solid slam. Then Loam climbed into the right side.

Mr. Moonbeam revved up the engine. He clicked on the radio to some talk show and cranked the volume.

I closed my eyes tight as we slowly backed up, the tires rolling over the weeds and grass.

I was on my way to Willis.

On my way to see Pop.

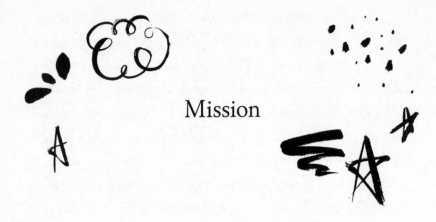

Mission

I was relieved when Mr. Moonbeam turned off the potholed road and onto the highway. My hand was hurting again, bad enough to scream the lungs out of my chest, but I sucked up the pain with deep, quiet breaths. I wondered what was going on inside G's head. I couldn't see her face, only her dirty sneakers and bare legs. She was probably thinking of all the laws in her black journal that we were breaking. Or maybe all the things that she *hadn't* written down as town record keeper since I'd been here, like finding Noreen's alcohol and Dandy's rainbow. I was proud of G though. She was as still as a boulder. She was one good stowaway.

I noticed a narrow scar on G's shin, and I knew that soon I'd probably end up with a serious scar on my hand and wrist from this burn. Pop had a bunch of tiny polka-dot scars on the back of his calves. I asked him once how he got them, and he said he was attacked by a blackberry bush when he was a kid. I wasn't too sure I believed him, though. It didn't seem like blackberry prickles would leave marks like that. Maybe I needed to come up with my own blackberry-attack story since I wasn't planning on telling anyone the *real* truth about my scar.

"We'll be lugging in the summer annuals this morning, Loam. This was a good day for you to join me," Mr. Moonbeam said. "Why didn't Dandy come?"

"Oh," Loam said.

I hoped his brain had woken up and he would have a good answer to that.

"Well, I just . . ."

"You needed a break. I dig."

I was glad his pop didn't need an explanation. This plan was working like a lucky charm.

They didn't talk much more. Mr. Moonbeam switched the radio to a station that played all rock songs, and he and Loam sang along. When I felt the old car slow, I knew we were getting close. Finally, we stopped, and Mr. Moonbeam turned off the engine.

"I gotta put my boots on, Dad, so I'll meet you by the loading truck, okay?"

I heard the car door slam, and then Loam said, "You can get up now. He's gone."

G exhaled long and loud, lifting the blanket off her frizzy head. I pulled myself onto the back seat and rolled my neck a bit.

"You two okay?" he said.

"Just stiff and hot." G moaned.

"You know where we are, right, Jane?" Loam asked. "The Willis nursery?"

"Of course. This is a good spot. It's not too far from the hospital."

Loam opened his door. "Okay, make sure you are back and hidden by four."

"Hey, Loam. Thanks," I said.

He gave me a fist bump as G and I climbed out of the back seat. I felt a little dizzy when I stood, and a burst of pain in my hand made me lean over and grab the side of the car.

G put her palm on my back. "What's wrong?"

"Nothing," I lied. "I just crawled out too fast. I'm fine."

When I felt all the swishy dizziness leave, I led G along Bandon Street. Today, I was the tour guide.

We passed the side street where Pop and I lived. "Look, G." I pointed toward the second house from the corner. "That's my house."

It didn't look at all like the tidy cabins in Three Boulders. The paint was a shabby, faded blue, the roof had a few missing shingles, and moss grew everywhere. Pop did the best he could with our little house, keeping the lawn mowed and the driveway swept, and all that important, good neighbor stuff. A year ago when we moved in, he had to rebuild the cracked porch steps. He taught me how to put the screwdriver heads in his drill. I loved that whirring sound of the drill and how those screws twisted straight into the wood. Just last month, Pop put a pot of petunias next to the door, which I helped him plant. Right now, those purple petunias didn't look so great.

"That's where I'll be in just seven more days, if I can talk to Pop."

"I'm not sure where I'll be in seven more days." G sighed.

"Chin up, G. We're collecting money, remember? Three Boulders is going to be saved."

I knew G's frizzy-headed brain hadn't stopped worrying about leaving Three Boulders, but I couldn't think any more about that today. I took one last glance at my house. As long as I had a chance to talk to Pop and get our story straight, I'd be back with him in that little house next week. Then I could water those sorry petunias.

"Jane! A police car!" G hollered.

I grabbed her arm and we ducked behind a small hedge next to the sidewalk. The cruiser floated past us, but I couldn't see the driver to find out if it was Officer D. I made sure it was well out of sight before I stood up. "Come on. Let's move."

Ten minutes later, we arrived at the hospital. Automatic glass doors opened for us. G stayed close by my side, but her head turned up, down, left and right, still searching for cops.

"Where do we go?" G asked.

Actually, I wasn't sure. There was a sign between the two elevators listing the important hospital places.

G walked toward it, pressing her pointy finger on the glass, moving it up and down the two lists.

"I don't see Rehab anywhere, Jane. There's Radiation, Reproductive Health, Respiratory Therapy, but no Rehab."

I was doing my own search of the board. "There it is." I pointed.

"'New Paradise Clinic'?" G read aloud.

"Yep. That's it. Third floor. Suite 327."

"How do you know that's it?"

"Because they don't call these places *rehab centers*. They always give them fancy, dreamy names, like Hope by the Ocean or Lakeshore Oasis. Names that make you think you're on a vacation or something."

"Oh." G followed me into the elevator. "I guess that makes sense."

When the doors slid open, we stepped out and made our way toward suite 327. The waiting room of the New Paradise Clinic smelled like the pine trees surrounding Three Boulders. There was a long hallway off the waiting room, and I wondered if Pop was somewhere in a room down that hall.

"Excuse me," I said to the lady at the counter. She wore a blue scarf around her head and had speckled green glasses that she peered over to look at me.

"May I help you?" she asked.

"I'm looking for my pop."

She took her glasses off and moved her hands away from the keyboard. "Did you get separated from him? I can have the hospital public address system help you locate him."

"No." I shook my head. "He's right here in the New Paradise Clinic."

The lady adjusted the scarf on her head. She whispered to me, "Sweetheart, I'm not allowed to verify if your father is a patient here, and even if he was, he's not allowed to have visitors."

I knew that perfectly well. That was the case at every clinic. The truth was that I'd never had the urgent need to see Pop while he was in rehab . . . until now.

It was time to work some serious charm on this lady. "My name is Jane," I began. "My pop is Jeremiah Pengilly. He's been here since Saturday night. He's a real nice man. You've probably met him, pretty tall and thin with reddish-brown hair that's a bit grown out right now, unless he got a haircut here." I checked her eyes for a reaction, but she was only looking at me with a pleasant, TV-ad smile.

"I just need to talk to my pop real quick. Don't worry, I'm not contaminated or anything. No bugs or head lice or anything like that, just a bandaged hand." I lifted my arm to show her.

She smiled again. "I'm sorry, sweetie. I wish I could help you."

"Please? It's terribly important that I see him. Please?" I felt G's arm on my back.

Right then I heard several voices. One sounded just like Pop. I turned my head, but I couldn't see anyone. The unhelpful desk lady stood up. "Excuse me for a moment." She walked through the white door to the right of her desk.

I glanced down the empty hallway and whispered to G. "Stay here and cover for me. I'll be back."

G gripped my good hand like a vise. Worry was seeping out of her skin. "Be careful."

I tiptoed down the hallway, turning doorknobs as I went. The first one was locked. So was the second. I crept toward the third door and turned the knob, hearing the release of the latch.

I had the door open just a tiny inch when I heard desk lady say, "You're not allowed back there."

Oh, serious crud!

I slowly walked back to the counter. G mouthed "sorry" to me.

"I was just trying to find a restroom," I fibbed.

Desk lady sat down. "I'm sorry that I can't help you." She rummaged through a drawer and grabbed something. "If you go back to the main hallway and turn right, there are restrooms four doors down, and here are some quarters. Treat yourself to something in the vending machine. It's just outside the door." She dropped a handful of quarters on the counter, but I was too disappointed to even bother grabbing them.

G and I stepped into the hallway. I suddenly didn't feel so hot. My head was swirly and swishy like it had been earlier, and my wrist was once again throbbing and burning. I leaned against the wall and lowered myself to the floor, squeezing my eyes shut.

"Now what?" G asked, scooting down next to me, but I didn't answer. "Jane? Are you okay?"

I wasn't okay at all. I thought it would be easy to see Pop for just a moment, to learn what had spilled from his mouth about that night. My brain was flitting around like a fly caught in a jar. What had he told social services Fran? Why did she need more time to investigate? My brain flitted back to that night, to Pop's face in the kitchen, to that look he gave me, that look of . . . No. No. I couldn't think about that. I pushed my hand hard against my belly. It was hurting worse than ever.

"Is it your hand? Do you need some help?"

I shoved my other hand in my pocket. "No, I'll be fine."

I tried one of those Three Boulders silent prayers. I prayed that everything would be fine for both me and Pop.

My eyes were pinched closed when I heard the voice.

The best voice in the world.

The only voice my ears wanted to hear.

Pop's voice.

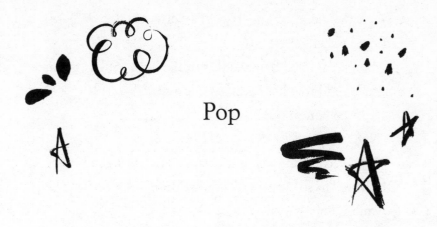

Pop

"Jane Girl?"

I looked in the direction of the voice. It really was Pop, dressed in his torn jeans and a black T-shirt. He was less than twenty feet away from me, standing in front of the vending machine. Forgetting my pain and dizziness, I sprang up and raced to Pop. I flung my arms around his belly, inhaling his cinnamon-grassy smell.

"Pop," I said, squeezing him tighter. That silent prayer really worked.

I felt him kiss my hair. His scruffy whiskers tickled my forehead. He wiggled my arms away from his waist and held my shoulders. "I swore I heard your voice inside the clinic. What're you doing here? Are you okay?"

"I wanted to see you, Pop. You look good." And he really did, just a little bit of sagginess around his eyeballs.

"Jane, you're not supposed to be here." He glanced

toward the door of the New Paradise Clinic. "Where's Officer Dashell?"

"She's . . ." I had to make this sound legit. "She's visiting a friend, and I told her I was getting a soda."

Not the honest truth.

Not at all.

Pop reached for my bum hand. His eyes got watery. "Oh, Jane, I'm so very sorry. I didn't mean—"

"Shhh, Pop. It's going to be okay."

"Are you in a lot of pain?"

"Nah." I was becoming a real professional at hiding pain, but right now, there were things way more important to discuss. I knew I didn't have much time.

"Pop?" I peeked over my shoulder. G was still sitting against the wall, watching us, but there was no one else in the hallway. "What did you say to Fran about that night?"

Pop let go of my hand. "I'm a little unclear on that night. It's hard to wrap my brain around it."

"Pop, listen. This is what happened." I reached up and pulled his uncombed head lower, so I could whisper in his ear. Pop always had the best advice in the world, and I listened to him most all of the time, and I did what he said most all of the time, but right now, he needed to listen to me. Our stories had to be the same.

"It went down like this," I began. "You were resting on

the couch after work, like you always do. Then you heard me in the kitchen, so you joined me. You turned on some music, and we did our dinner-making dance. Then I just slipped. It was an accident. I fell against the stove, so you called nine-one-one. That's it."

"Is that really what happened?" He was staring at my arm again. "Jane Girl, did I—"

"Just say that, Pop. Say that, and we'll be back together faster than we can bomb Applegate Hill. Okay?"

He sighed and scratched his head.

I didn't want Pop to question me anymore, so I said, "That's G sitting down there. She's been real nice to me."

"And Officer Dashell? She's been good to you too?"

"She's been real good," I said.

Honest truth.

"And you're doing your schoolwork?"

"Yes. I think my TBS might be cured."

Pop glanced up the hall again and then whispered, "Jane Girl, I'm making us new longboards."

"You are?" I bounced on my toes.

"Yes. I got permission from my counselor. He agreed it was great therapy for me. I'm shaping our decks like fish. Mine's a salmon and yours is a trout." Pop was beaming.

"That's awesome!"

And I meant it. I couldn't wait to bomb hills on our

matching fish boards.

Pop put his finger to his lips and shushed me. "I can't afford new trucks and bearings yet. That will come later."

"Pop, you're the best." I held up my good hand for a high five. "I haven't boarded for six days. They don't have paved roads in this Three Boulders place." I paused. "It's really weird there. Wait 'til I tell you all about it."

Pop combed his fingers through his hair. "So . . . you've met Red Norton?"

I stepped back. "You know Old Red?"

Now Pop's eyes scrunched up and his head tilted. "I, uh . . ." But he didn't finish. He wrapped his arms around my shoulders and squeezed. "I'll explain everything to you when we're back together. I promise."

I wanted him to explain right this second. How could Pop know about Old Red?

But he peeled me off him and whispered, "I have to get back now, Jane. A meeting is starting. Go back to Officer Dashell."

"Remember what I told you." I squeezed his hand tight. "Just seven more days, Pop."

He winked at me. "Stay out of trouble."

"Of course."

I was trying to do that.

"We got this," I added.

"Of course."

Pop headed back to the entrance of the New Paradise Clinic.

I was feeling a gazillion times better after talking to him. My plan had worked perfectly thanks to G and Loam Moonbeam and my silent prayers. Now I was sure Pop would tell our story just like I told him to.

"I'm glad you got to see your pop," G said. We began walking down the hallway toward the elevators.

"Me too. He's making me a new longboard." There was a big grin on my face and she grinned back.

"So, everything is okay now?"

"Sure," I said, even though everything was not okay. My brain was still puzzled about Pop mentioning Old Red.

"Hey," I said, "let's go to the park. I can show you the skate ramps, and maybe we can find some coins. I always find coins in the park. We can add them to our Three Boulders collection."

The elevator doors opened and G and I stepped inside, pressing the lobby button. "Look," G said, opening her palm. "I grabbed those quarters the lady left on the front desk."

"You're as slick handed as Loam!"

"That's not funny," G said.

But what really wasn't funny was what we saw when the elevator doors opened.

Standing there in the hospital lobby, tapping her polished black shoe on the floor, gripping her walkie-talkie, and frowning, was none other than Officer Doris D. Dashell.

Crud, crud, crud!

Me and G were *so* busted.

The Ride Back to Three Boulders

I walked right to Officer D and held out both my wrists, preparing to get handcuffed.

She scowled at me. "Outside. Both of you." She wore her one-hundred-percent cop face. She was boiling-hot mad. I wondered if she would send me to a new foster home. Maybe I was too much trouble for her.

The hospital doors whooshed open, and Officer D marched to her cruiser. We followed. G's head dropped below her shoulders.

Last Sunday, when Officer D brought me to Three Boulders, I was secretly hoping that I would get a ride in her cop car. Now it was the last thing in the world I wanted.

"Do we have to sit in the back seat behind that window cage?" I asked, imagining people peering at us as we drove by, wondering what two girls could have done to be tossed in the back of a cop cruiser.

Officer D scowled again. "A part of me thinks you *should* sit back there." She shook her head. "You can both climb in the front seat."

G got in first. She was stony silent, just staring at the cruiser's dashboard.

"I don't know what you were thinking, Jane," Officer D said, slamming the driver's door.

What I was thinking was that Pop needed to get his story right.

What I was thinking was that social services Fran needed to stop questioning us and threatening to keep us apart.

Now I didn't know *what* would happen. Maybe I blew it. Maybe I won't get to ride my new trout longboard because *maybe* twelve days would become twelve . . . forevers.

I squeezed my eyelids to stop the rogue tear from dripping down my cheek.

Officer D took a deep breath. "You *knew* it wasn't possible to see your pop."

But I had seen him.

G's head rose a milli bit. Our eyeballs met.

"Do you know how much seeing and talking to your pop could have jeopardized the investigation?"

Me and G's eyeballs remained locked together.

Officer D didn't know.

She didn't know I *had* seen Pop.

Maybe I *hadn't* blown it.

"I do not know the details of how you managed to get into Willis this morning, but let me go over the laws you girls broke with this escapade. First, you came without parent or guardian permission. Second, you failed to complete your daily duties. Third, you lied about your whereabouts. Fourth . . ."

Officer D's cop words all ran together after a while. When she finally turned off her word faucet, I asked a question. "How'd you know we were here?"

I got a big eyebrow lift from her.

"Did either of you truly believe that in a community of fifty-six people, *no one* would figure out you were missing?"

We said nothing.

"There was a search of every cabin and all the surrounding area of Three Boulders once Mr. Biggs became suspicious. When you were not found, Mr. Norton contacted me. It didn't take advanced detective skills to figure out you would be at the hospital."

I crossed my arms over my belly, holding my bum hand tight. There was nothing else to say.

"We're really sorry, Officer Dashell. Really, really sorry," G said softly.

I knew G meant it.

But me? I wasn't really, really sorry. At least I wasn't sorry about sneaking out of Three Boulders because I *had* talked to Pop, and the only people who knew *that* truth were me and G.

I was sorry about G, though. About causing trouble for her.

And I was sorry I let down Officer D because the honest truth was that she was a good foster person.

She drove us all the way back to Three Boulders wearing her cop face.

I tried silent prayers to wash that face away, but those prayers didn't work too good.

Day Seven

Punishment

Me and G were told to report to Old Red at nine o'clock in the morning. I was prepared for some harsh punishment. I thought about the possibilities while I changed my bandage. I still didn't want Officer D to see all the disgusting greenish goobers. Maybe Old Red would tie us to chairs and guard us night and day like prisoners. Maybe he'd make us do hard labor for hours on end, like cleaning *all* the toilets and showers in Three Boulders. Maybe he'd shoot us in the toes.

I brought up this possibility with Officer D before breakfast.

"Good grief, Jane. He is not going to shoot you." She was *way* calmer this morning than she'd been yesterday, probably because for the last several hours I had been doing my best to be a good foster kid and follow her directions. I didn't want her mad at me anymore.

"Red Norton has the biggest heart of any man I've ever known. He will *not* shoot you. He will *not* harm you," Officer D insisted.

"How can you be so sure?"

"I just am," she said. "And also, I happen to know that there are no shots in his gun." She tapped her holster with her thick fingers. "This is the only loaded weapon in all of Three Boulders."

I still wasn't sure I believed Officer D, so just in case, I spent extra time getting myself ready so I looked presentable for my sentencing. I put on my last clean pair of cargo shorts, my favorite blue hoodie, and Pop's gray stocking cap. I washed my face, which was getting tan from all the boonieville outdoor time. I wiped the dirt off the edges of my shoes and brushed my teeth an extra ten seconds.

At breakfast, G didn't want to talk. Her face was blotchy and baggy like she had cried all night. Her hair was an awful frizzy mess. After we ate, we made our way to Old Red's cabin. G still hadn't said a word, not even a reminder for me to be polite. We sat down carefully, side by side, on his musty blue couch. Old Red faced us, sitting in a rocking chair.

There was a terribly long silence. It made my burned hand pulse with pain. I took a deep breath, trying to ignore the achiness.

"Gertrude and Jane," Old Red said, shotgun in hand

as always. "I don't intend to lecture you because you both know what you did was wrong."

That was relief to my ears.

"I also know that Officer Dashell spoke with you at length."

He sure got that right.

"I have considered numerous consequences for both of you"—I braced myself, pushing my shoulders back and sitting up taller—"and I have determined that neither of you will be able to play in tomorrow's softball game."

Huh?

Really?

That was it?

I was just about ready to leap off that couch and shake Old Red's hand in gratitude when G started to cry.

Actually, it wasn't even crying. She started to sob, as though Old Red had canceled Christmas or something *really* horrible like that. I elbowed her, but she just kept bawling.

I knew G loved softball, but it was just *one* game. Apparently her brain didn't understand how easy we got off.

G just kept crying, loud wails and fat tears that I was afraid might drown us if she didn't stop. I shot a glance at Old Red, but not one word came out of his mouth. I began to wonder if she was faking those tears.

But the thing was, if she was faking, she deserved one of those naked gold statues. This was good acting.

A funny feeling was growing inside me. If I hadn't come to Three Boulders, G wouldn't be here now, sobbing. Ever since I'd arrived, G had been helping me, being a friend, and being my teammate. Now I needed to be her friend.

"Mr. Norton," I said. "I'd like to negotiate with you."

"Would you?" he asked, his face stern.

"Yes . . ." I had to get this right. My brain thought about all the punishments Pop had handed me in my life. He always said the punishment needed to make sense, so I said to Old Red, "It doesn't really seem right to have us miss a softball game when we broke rules by sneaking into Willis. That would be like shooting us in the toes for getting an F on a spelling test."

I glanced at Old Red's gun. Maybe that was a bad example.

"I think it would make more sense for me and G to play a little catch-up."

"Catch-up?"

"Have us do everything we were supposed to do yesterday, like help wash some dishes, complete our schoolwork, *and* have us do all our chores today as well. We could even pluck a few more weeds from the garden beds. Then, if we finish, maybe we can play in that softball game tomorrow."

I knew that this offer was going to involve more work than I normally did in a whole week, and I didn't know if it was even humanly possible to do two days of work in one, but G was no longer crying, and that relieved my brain.

"That's a very logical offer, young Jane." Old Red rocked slowly back and forth. "You remind me of my daughter, Florence. She was a feisty one and a quick thinker. Two qualities that often got her in trouble, but just as often got her *out* of trouble."

I peered at Old Red's face. I remembered how Officer D said he had an enormous heart. I wasn't sure it was enormous, but I was beginning to see that at least he *had* a heart inside that skinny chest.

"I accept your offer, Jane," he said.

"Oh, thank you, Mr. Norton!" G sprang from the couch and leaned over his rocking chair and kissed his wrinkly cheek.

I was not going to kiss Old Red Norton, but I did smile at him.

The Old Blue Journal

As soon as we left Old Red's cabin, our day of slavery began. We started in Noreen's kitchen. She asked us to clean the oven racks, but she quickly realized I couldn't soak my bum hand in water or use it to scrub, so G did all the scrubbing, and I just wiped the racks dry when she was done. Next we pulled weeds from the garden beds. Preston Farmer loomed over me pointing out all the pea-size weeds.

"G," I said. My hand was throbbing, so I took a break and sat on the edge of the garden bed. "What's up with this softball game tomorrow? Why is it so important to you?"

"It's important to everyone, not just me," G said. "This could be our very last game ever. We have a long history of softball in Three Boulders. We've played almost twelve hundred games over the past fifty years, and the details of every game have been recorded. Would you like to see all the softball journals?"

"Um . . . that's tempting, but I'll pass."

"If the Royal Hitters beat the Mighty Catchers tomorrow, they will have the longest winning streak in history."

"Which team are you on?"

"The Hitters. Officer Dashell is a Royal Hitter too. Winning tomorrow means she would be part of *another* Three Boulders softball record. Can you believe that?" G gushed.

In my seven days in Three Boulders, I'd discovered you can believe just about anything.

"And since you're her guest, you'll be on our team too." G beamed at me. She was a softball-loving soul.

I tugged at the bandage on my hand. It was getting loose, probably from all the work I had done today.

"Thanks for what you said to Mr. Norton about negotiating our punishment," G said.

"You're welcome."

The honest truth was that the extra work hadn't been horrible.

After Preston Farmer inspected our weeding, we headed down to the shady church fire pit to cool off and work on our nature project. Loam and Dandy were leaning against a log pew, side by side, on the dirt when we arrived. Dandy saw us first and she jumped up and squeezed us both around our bellies at the same time.

Loam stood up too. "Hey. I want you to know that I

worked really hard not to rat on you. My dad got a phone call at the nursery, and then he started asking me questions. At first I said nothing, but then he started to say how worried folks were and how they were afraid something bad would happen to you both, and . . ." He kicked the log with his beat-up sandal. "So I told them you hid in the back of the car, but that's *all* I said. I didn't say anything about going to see your pop, Jane."

G straddled a pew log and sat down. "I believe you, Loam."

I thought he could have kept his mouth completely shut and not said anything at all. He hid Dandy's rainbow secret for a long time. He could have held mine.

"Loam, when are you going to return all that stuff?" G asked.

Loam touched Dandy's shoulder. "We've been working on a plan. Dandy understands that everything has to go back. We actually started today. We returned a few things to the dining hall, some dishes and such."

Weed girl clapped her hands.

"We have a few things for both of you." He handed me Pop's orange stocking cap, and he gave G a green writing pen.

"I put the bottle of alcohol back, so don't worry about that anymore. And I have one more thing." He leaned over and picked up the old blue People of Three Boulders journal. He held it out to G.

G put her palm up, stopping Loam. "You need to put that back where you found it, with all the other old journals."

He began flipping the pages of the blue journal. "But I was glancing through it, and I think you both need to see something."

"No," G said firmly. "It's not mine." She slapped the journal closed, holding down Loam's hand.

"It's just that there's some information in here that—"

"No, Loam."

He didn't move his hand away from G's, but he looked toward *me* with laser eyeballs.

"I don't want anything to do with stolen goods or information from stolen goods. That's final," G said. "Put the journal back, Loam."

He nodded and stood up slowly. The journal remained in his hand. G was right. He did need to return it, but my brain was curious about what Loam had seen inside.

As Loam and Dandy began to walk away, he turned and looked at me again. I swear his eyeballs were trying to tell me something important.

What was it?

Day Eight

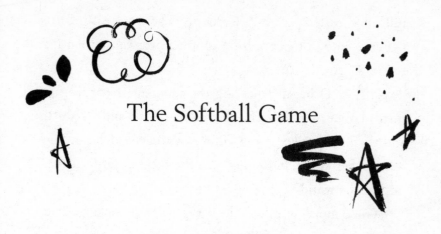

The Softball Game

The morning of the big softball game, I woke up sweaty and shaky. My hand ached like sharp teeth were biting into my flesh. I sat up on the couch, but dizziness made me lie right back down. I unwound my bandage and had to turn my head to the side to catch my breath because my arm smelled yucky. Today there were red streaks shooting from the bend of my wrist almost up to my elbow.

For a short moment, I thought about waking Officer D and letting her know I wasn't doing too good, but if she knew how bad I was hurting, she might take me to the doctor, and then social services Fran might find out, and she might force me to answer *more* questions about that night. All I needed was to get through these last five days, get back to Pop, and never have to think about that night or my hand again.

I sipped some water, took another one of those pain

pills, and rested for a bit. Carefully, I rewrapped my arm being sure to put extra white goop all over those shooting red rays.

Officer D began whistling the moment she woke up. Instead of her cop uniform, she put on sweats and a T-shirt, and then she yanked a red visor down over her head. She opened her closet and pulled out the biggest darn softball mitt in the world.

"Good morning, Jane." She was practically singing. "Are you ready to be part of Three Boulders history and break a record today?" She spun her mitt on her pointer finger.

It was a good thing she was so distracted because she didn't even comment on how my bandage was wrapped almost to my elbow or how I was sitting so still on the couch.

Crud, it was hurting bad.

But seeing her this excited about the game made me even more certain. I could *not* mention my hand. I couldn't make her miss this game.

"Jane," Officer D said, "you're not going to be able to wear a mitt at the game today. I was thinking that you could be the Hitters number one cheerleader."

A flood of relief gushed through my whole body. I wasn't sure I could even stand up, let alone swing a bat or catch a softball.

"I don't have to wear some dumb skirt and shake my booty the whole game, do I?"

"No skirts and no booty shaking, Jane. You just have to lead some cheers, nice and loud. Dandy will cheer with you."

Actually, that sounded like something I could do—be nice and loud, I mean. Even as cruddy as I was feeling, loudness came pretty natural to me.

At eleven o'clock, all fifty-six humans in Three Boulders trekked to the softball diamond. About half sat in the rickety bleachers, talking and eating popcorn. Officer D told me to just relax in the Hitters dugout during warm-ups, which I was happy to do. Dandy sat next to me, and that was perfect because I knew she wouldn't ask any questions.

G came into the dugout at one point, rattling off the positions and the batting order to me. When I didn't respond, she looked right into my eyes. "Jane, does your hand hurt?"

"A little." That was a universe-size lie. "Don't worry about me, G. Just get out there and win the game."

Old Red, the umpire, sat in a fold-up chair right behind the wire backstop. Every so often, he looked my way. G told me he knew every word in the official softball rule book.

I believed that.

When Old Red blew his whistle, the Mighty Catchers stayed on the field, and the Royal Hitters jogged to their dugout.

G was our leadoff hitter. The crowd started hollering at her, "Hey, batter, batter!"

It was time to start my official role as cheerleader. I stood next to the dugout fence, leaning against the metal pole, and chanted for my friend:

G, G, she's our man!
If she can't do it, no one can!
Go, G!
Go, G!

I waved a mitt with my good hand over my head like a pom-pom. Dandy flapped her hands over her head.

Preston Farmer, the Three Boulders strikeout record holder, stood on the pitching mound. He looked all business up there, and he stared at G, who held her bat high and pinched her lips tight. He swung his arm in a circle and fired a pitch to his catcher.

"Strike!" Old Red yelled.

"C'mon, G!" I cheered.

Preston launched another pitch.

"Strike two!"

G tapped her bat on the dirt a few times and then lifted it high again.

Preston Farmer hurled the third pitch, and G took a

whopping swing and smacked that ball deep into center field. She sprinted all the way to second base.

"You rock, G!" I hollered.

That was the first hit of many for the Royal Hitters. As the game went on, they continued to slug that ball left and right, and runners crossed home plate almost every inning. G was awesome. She made some great catches at second base, and I hollered my lungs out for her, doing my best job as team cheerleader.

Then there was Officer D. She hit a home run her first time at bat, and in a later inning, one of the Catchers smacked a line drive right in her thigh, but she hardly even flinched. She just scooped it off the ground and tossed it to third base for an out. The Hitters were rolling toward the record books.

By the last inning, players weren't sitting in their dugouts anymore. They lined the sides of the field, clapping and hollering at teammates. I was still doing my best to cheer because that was my job, after all.

Even though I felt like a pile of doggie doo, I noticed everyone around me. The Hitters had grins from earlobe to earlobe. The Catchers were fist-bumping and pumping up their teammates. Folks on the bleachers were whistling and stomping their feet. Every Three Boulderite was excited. I was all swept up in their fun, and I felt a smile rising inside me just being with them, together in a big group, cheering each other along. I'd never done anything like this with Pop. We only had each other to cheer for.

"Jane!" G waved her arm over her head. "You get to play now!"

Oh no.

G jogged toward me. "We like everyone to play at least one inning. We're up by three runs. I think the game is ours!" she said. "Here's a right-handed mitt for your good hand. If a ball comes your way, catch it with the mitt, transfer the ball to your left hand, shake off the mitt and then, throw the ball directly to me, okay?"

That was an awful lot of directions.

I glanced at Officer D, hoping to see her shake her head and maybe yell at me to sit back down and cheer, but she gave me a thumbs-up and pointed to right field.

"Come on, Jane!" Loam yelled.

The Hitters actually *wanted* me to play.

This was not good news, but I couldn't let my new teammates down, and I had to keep everyone believing that I was doing just fine and that my skin didn't feel sticky and my head wasn't burning up, and my legs weren't wobbling. I made my way to the outfield, and as I was walking, I decided to try a little prayer. Maybe in Three Boulders, at this important softball game, God might listen. Maybe he would help end this game quickly.

I kept my eye and ear on Old Red, watching his arm motions, calling strikes and balls. So far there were two outs and no one on base. This was good. God *was* listening. G was hopping like a wild rabbit near second base. It was definitely looking like the Hitters would get that win-streak record.

But then things went downhill—real fast. First Preston Farmer got on base. Then Chef Noreen had a hit, and then Mrs. Biggs and all her frizzy hair smacked that softball right between G and Loam. The bases were loaded for the Catchers.

My heart and knees relaxed, though, when I saw who was up next: little Timmy Spencer. There was no way in a whole lifetime of Three Boulders softball games that he could get a hit and give the Mighty Catchers the lead.

Sure enough, Timmy swung hard on Alan Stein's first two pitches. I started walking toward G, getting ready to celebrate, when a third pitch was thrown. Timmy flung that bat and slapped the ball like a peewee-size Babe Ruth . . . right in my direction.

Oh crud, crud!

I backpedaled, feeling my heart pound. Back and back I moved, but that ball just kept soaring. It kind of turned into slow motion as I watched it fly farther and farther until eventually, it dropped and hit the ground way beyond me and just behind a line drawn with white chalk over the grass.

Little muscleman Timmy Spencer had hit a home run. All those push-ups paid off. This was probably a new Three Boulders record.

Pop always told me that when a person does a real amazing thing, you've got to let them know because everyone needs pats on the back. Timmy Spencer hitting a home run, yep, *that* was amazing.

So I put on my cheerleader voice and hollered, "Woohoo, Timmy!"

I didn't need to know much about softball to be able to add up those numbers. I was a good adder, after all. The Catchers had just won the game.

Every member of the Royal Hitters squad was furious. Our pitcher, Alan Stein, threw his glove to the dirt. G kicked her feet, spreading dirt all over second base. Officer D punched her fist into her mitt. I was the only Hitter cheering for Timmy. I cheered for him as he jumped on first base right next to Officer D and then skipped on toward second, and then, before I could let out one more whoop, Timmy was lying in the dirt, rolling in a ball, clutching his ankle.

Officer D got to him first. She leaned down and placed her man paws on his ankle. "He's hurt!" she said.

"I gotta run!" Timmy shrieked. He tried to roll over and stand, but his mom got to him and held him down with Officer D.

"Sweetheart, you don't have to run."

"I gotta run the bases!" Timmy screamed again.

"You hit the winning home run, Timmy. You won the game for the Catchers!" his mom said.

"Technically, the lad is correct, Amelia." Old Red was inching toward the small crowd that gathered around Timmy. "He does need to run the bases or his home run won't count."

"That's ridiculous, Red," Mrs. Spencer said. "He's hurt. He can't possibly run."

"Rules are rules, I'm afraid," Old Red said.

"I can do it," Timmy squeaked, and he tried to push himself up and stand on his ankle, but he just collapsed right back onto the ground. I felt sorry for him. One moment he was the hero and the next moment, he was . . .

"This is crazy," Preston Farmer said. He walked right up to Timmy and lifted him in his arms. "I'll carry him around the bases."

"Preston, I have read the rule book of softball from cover to cover. A teammate cannot be carried," Old Red said. "We made a pact here in Three Boulders that the rules of the game will be abided by at all times. We can't make an exception now."

Grumblings sprang up from everywhere, a tornado of whistles, cheers, and boos. All the laws in this place made my brain hurt. They should know that sometimes there has to be exceptions. Timmy Spencer deserved an exception.

So I said, nice and clear, "I'll carry him."

Everyone heard me. I know they did because the tornado died to an eerie calm, with every set of Three Boulder eyeballs locked on me.

"Didn't you hear what Red said? He can't be carried." Preston Farmer peered at me.

"I heard him. He said Timmy couldn't be carried by a *teammate*." I paused. "Well, I'm not a teammate. Timmy's a Catcher and I'm a Hitter."

That eerie calm continued as everyone digested my words.

"Timmy, if you can stand on your good leg, I think you can hop on my back, and I'll give you a piggyback ride," I said, reaching for his arm.

Officer D was standing with her fists on her wide hips, her chin hung low. G looked like she wanted to cry.

"Red, are you going to let this happen?" Alan Stein was not happy.

Old Red had a crooked, wrinkly smile on his face. "Alan, there's no rule that says an *opposing* player cannot carry the runner around the bases."

"Great." I said. "C'mon, Timmy, hop on."

Timmy slowly rose and managed to climb on my back. He was pretty heavy for a peewee, and I had to take a deep breath to keep my balance. I walked slowly toward second base. I squatted down so he could tap the base with his toe to make it official. I clung to him with both hands which made the bandage twist and grind into my burned skin.

Crikity crud, that hurt.

But I kept moving around the bases, grimacing, gripping Timmy's skinny legs. I think I dropped him onto home plate. I'm not really sure because the dirt and the backstop and all the cheering people were getting fuzzy and jumbled in my brain.

But I do remember screaming.

And I was pretty sure that if there was a Three Boulders record for the loudest, shrillest scream ever emitted, I broke that record right then and there at the softball game.

Day Nine

Gifts from Three Boulders

When my eyelids cracked open, the first thing I noticed were pasty green walls surrounding me. I closed my eyes again and wiggled my piggy toes from the little ones to the big ones. My brain was waking up, and I had some memories. Little snippets of pictures formed, one at a time, but together, they didn't make much sense.

I remembered being lifted off the ground. Timmy Spencer had his hands squeezed over his ears. G whispered something to me. Someone held my good arm, telling me I was really brave, and that I would be fine. There was a squirrel on Officer D's truck. A blond lady with furry kittens on her shirt said, "This will pinch."

I opened my eyelids again. The pasty walls were still there, but this time, I noticed tubes. One tube went into the top of my good hand, held down with smooth white tape and the other tube led to the inside of my elbow. My burned hand rested on my belly, wrapped real snug with an ugly brown bandage, clear up beyond my funny bone. It didn't hurt one bit. I wiggled my piggy toes again, just to make sure I had feeling in my body. I wiggled my fingers too. They all moved.

I was definitely alive in this pasty green room.

"Good morning, Jane." It was the same voice I'd been hearing for the last eight days, Officer D.

I couldn't quite get any words out, which made me question once more whether I was really alive. Just in case, I wiggled my fingers again.

A man with flying hippos on his shirt moved toward me. He said a bunch of stuff about how nice it was to see the blue of my eyes, and that he was going to take my blood pressure and check my temperature. I stared and stared at those flying hippos as my arm was twisted and squeezed.

Next there was a stick shoved in my mouth, and then a disk placed on my chest, and while flying hippo man and Officer D were talking, my brain had a few more pictures flash into my memory. First it was sound, the tinny rattle of a car door slamming. Then it was a feeling, a seat belt strapping across my chest. Then the picture changed. I was sitting on the kitchen floor, *my* kitchen floor. Pop was next to me. I could hear him. *Jane Girl, what have I done?*

Flying hippo man put both his hands on my neck and pressed lightly, and that's when my voice came back.

"Pop?" I asked. "Where's Pop?"

Officer D sat down in a chair next to me. She touched my shoulder. "He's not here, Jane. Remember, he's at the clinic."

"Can he come see me?"

Officer D shook her head. Her hand was still on my shoulder.

"Why do I have these tubes in me?"

"Your wound is badly infected. The tubes are feeding you antibiotics and some pain medication too." She took a deep breath and looked at the floor. "I can't believe I didn't see how sick you were, Jane. I should arrest myself for not noticing." She took another breath. "You were hiding your pain from me, weren't you?"

I didn't say a word.

"Jane." Officer D picked up my hand with the tubes and squeezed it. "I have to ask you, is there anything else you've been hiding? Do you have something more to tell me about that night?"

I swallowed hard. My mouth felt dry and crackly. Officer D handed me a paper cup with a straw and I sipped some water. "No," I said.

She sighed, then leaned back in the chair, still holding my hand. "Okay," she said softly, and she gave me her worried look. "Do you remember what happened yesterday?"

"A bit."

Officer D recapped the softball game, how I helped Timmy earn his home run, and how happy all the Mighty Catchers were and how much they praised me, and then how I screamed in pain and how she carried me all the way to her truck and rushed me to the hospital.

"Are you mad at me?" I asked.

"Why would I be mad?" She touched my chin, that sort of parentish thing she does.

"Because I lost the game for the Hitters, and you didn't get the win-streak record."

Officer D leaned forward, and I think there was a little tear growing inside one of her eyeballs. I wasn't real sure, though, because the pasty green walls were still making my vision fuzzy.

"Jane, I may have been a little upset at that moment, but what you did was the greatest display of sportsmanship I have ever seen in my lifetime. You should be in the record books for that. I am nothing but proud of you."

She reached down and pulled out a red softball visor from a large gift bag. She stuck it on my head. "You're a true Hitter now, Jane." She smiled at me.

"Red Norton was proud too. He sent something for you." She leaned over the gift bag again and brought out a softball with the signatures of every person in Three Boulders and set it on my belly. I gazed at that ball with the fifty-six signatures.

This was better than a gold medal or a shiny trophy.

"And here is a thank-you card from Timmy." Officer D held up the card so I could see the picture Timmy had drawn of me with his colored markers. I was a stick figure with a big blob on one arm that looked like a bowling ball. There was another stick figure on my back.

Next she unwrapped a frosted pink doughnut with mounds of sprinkles that Chef Noreen had made special just for me. Then there was a get-well note from Loam with a drawing of a rainbow that Dandy had added. Preston Farmer sent a packet of cucumber seeds and the Stein family sent a bouquet of flowers from the front of their cabin. Officer D placed them in a glass on my hospital tray.

"What about G?" I asked. "Is she upset? She wanted to win that game real bad."

"She just wants you to get better." Officer D grabbed two last things from the bag, a red journal and a card. "These are from her. She wrote down all the details from the softball game in that journal. She thought you might like to read about it."

I asked Officer D to take out G's card. There was a photo of the three boulders on the front, Redemption, Forgiveness, and Community. The rocks glowed like stony angel figures, like maybe God himself was hovering right on top of them, watching over every person in that family-like community. I wasn't going to admit this out loud to Officer

D or anyone else, but I realized that maybe Three Boulders wasn't as crazy of a place as I first believed.

But I still thought the boulders had stupid names.

Officer D opened the card, and I silently read G's words:

> *I am so glad I met you. I know you want to get back to your pop, but I wish you could stay in Three Boulders. I wish I could stay too. I will never forget you, Jane Pengilly. You will be my friend forever. Get well soon. Love, G*

Those might have been the best words I'd ever read. I gazed at the picture of those rocks again, and then I hugged the card and picture tight against my chest.

Day Ten

Old Red's Story

I woke up when I felt that familiar squeezing around my arm. It was flying hippo man once again taking my blood pressure, but today he was ice cream cone man. Those cones on his shirt looked good enough to eat. I wondered if they were feeding me enough in this hospital because right now, I was hungry enough to eat his whole *shirt*. Ice cream would sure taste good now. Pop gave me ice cream for breakfast once. It was the morning after I took a big tumble off my longboard bombing Applegate Hill. Pop said that ice cream was almost like medicine because you always felt better when you ate it.

The surprising thing was I didn't even have to ask for ice cream because a voice said, "Perhaps a frothy chocolate milk shake would be good for the patient this morning."

The voice wasn't hippo ice cream man and it wasn't Pop. It was Old Red Norton. He was perched in the chair next to my bed, arms crossed over his button-down shirt and jacket, his crinkly red ears sticking out like usual.

Hippo ice cream man nodded. "Fantastic idea. I'll go order that." He set the clipboard in a slot at the end of my bed. "You're doing well, Jane. Looks like you'll be going home tomorrow."

No, I'd be going back to Three Boulders tomorrow. I'd be going to my *real* home in three days. My pop.

Hippo ice cream man left the room, and I got a tiny tingle in my belly knowing that I was alone with Old Red for the very first time.

"Where's Officer D?" I asked.

"She had a lot of work to do today so she asked me to come visit you. I'll be checking out my new apartment later this afternoon too."

He had a black cane wedged between his legs.

"Where's your gun?"

"I can't bring a shotgun into a hospital, Jane."

That made sense, and I was glad about that too. "Officer D told me your gun isn't loaded. Why do you carry it around?"

Old Red settled into the back of his chair. "That's a long story. One I suppose we should talk about."

"Did you shoot someone?"

"Hmm . . ." he said.

"You can tell me. I'm good at keeping secrets."

That was the honest truth.

"All right. I'll tell you the story, Jane." He raised his cane and gently set it across his lap.

Hippo ice cream man returned and held out my milk shake. I took a big slurp through the straw. It was sweet and creamy and made my insides chilly. I held the cup and shifted in the bed so I could listen to Old Red's story.

"My parents died of the influenza when I was a young man, just twenty years old," he began. "I took it hard."

"I'm sorry," I said, and I really was 'cause I knew that losing my own pop would hurt more than any pain I felt from my burned hand.

"They owned a peach orchard down in California, and when they died, the orchard was left to my brother and me, but I didn't like running the orchard. Didn't like dealing with the pickers, the pests that ate our fruit, the money issues. It wasn't the life I wanted. But also . . ." He paused. His voice got softer. "Also I was drinking a lot."

I let out a big exhale. I definitely knew about drinking a lot.

"So I made a decision to start over. I left California with my wife, Eleanor."

"Pop says that moving to a new place builds character."

"Well, I certainly needed to build my character. You see, before I left, I packed up the load of cash that my father stored under the floorboards below his dresser. Half of that cash was my brother's. I took it all." Sadness sagged in his cheeks.

"Oh," I said. That was stealing.

Even though I knew what he had done was a bad thing, I felt sorry for him. "I guess you left him the peaches."

"Yes. I left him the peaches and the land, and I can't tell you how many times I've wondered what he did with it."

"You didn't ask him?"

Old Red shook his head. "I never saw him again." He swallowed hard.

I let him gulp on his sad memories a bit, but then I asked, "So then you found Three Boulders and decided to live there?"

"Not exactly. Three Boulders seemed to find me."

"Rocks can't find people."

Old Red laughed.

I wasn't trying to be funny, but I was glad some of his sadness lifted away.

"Seeing those boulders the first time sparked something in me," he said. "I knew that this was where I wanted to live. This was my refuge, and I wanted my children to run around the fir trees and climb on those boulders, and my grandchildren and my great-grandchildren." Old Red stopped talking for a bit. He eyed me while I slurped my milk shake.

"Is that when you made up all the weird laws?" I asked him.

"There was no need for laws right away. Eleanor and I were the only ones who lived there."

I set my milk shake cup on the rolling tray, wondering when the shooting part of this story was going to begin.

Old Red rambled on. "One day a man by the name of Ellis Grigsby wandered into Three Boulders."

"Wandered in?" That seemed strange because there wasn't even a road into Three Boulders.

"He wandered in straight from the county jail."

"A convict!" This was getting more interesting.

"He asked for a meal and he offered to build me a shed in exchange for more meals." Old Red paused. "Eventually, he asked if he could build a house for himself, and I said yes. Eleanor liked having him around."

"But he was a criminal! What did he do?"

"I never asked him. Honestly, it didn't matter to me. He was a hard worker, and I could tell he had a good heart. Sometimes, you just know these things. Sometimes you know that a person needs space and time to sort through problems."

I knew that real well, 'cause that's exactly what Pop needed—space and time to sort through his problems, for twelve days.

"So that's when Three Boulders began to grow. We invited a few folks we had met down in Willis to live with us, folks we knew needed a little calmness in their lives.

Our daughter, Florence, was born too. We all became a community, an extended family, sharing meals, working on the land together, pooling our resources. But most important, we accepted everyone's strengths and weaknesses."

"But you still haven't told me about your shotgun. Did you actually *shoot* someone?"

Old Red's stare dug into my brain. "Folks had been seeing some mountain lions in the area, so I began carrying that gun as a precaution."

I nodded, urging him to continue, happy to finally get to the good part.

"But here's the thing, young Jane. As much as I enjoyed being in Three Boulders and building this community, I was still drinking. I couldn't seem to stop."

I understood that well.

Too well.

Old Red had an ogre like Pop.

"Drinking and toting a gun around is just a bad thing to do," he continued. "About thirty-some years ago, I was sitting on the porch of the dining hall. It was calm and dusky and I heard a noise. At first it sounded like a person, but then in my liquored-up state, I thought it was a hiss. I stood up, and there across the road, I saw glowing eyes, just about the height of a mountain lion," he paused. "I propped that gun on my shoulder and I waited, watching those eyes, making sure. When I heard another hiss, I fired."

"Did you get the mountain lion?"

"No," he said. "After I fired, I heard a scream, and it wasn't a wild animal's scream. It was a little boy. I had shot a little boy."

I gasped. "Did he die?"

He shook his head back and forth, and finally he said, "No. The shots hit his leg in several places, but he recovered from the wounds." He huffed out a big tired sigh and said softly, "I'm not sure I've fully recovered though."

I looked at the wrinkles on the ancient dude's cheeks. Nine days ago when I met him, those wrinkles seemed to squeeze out something frightening, something I thought I should be afraid of. But now I saw how they just carried the pain and worry of his past. I wondered if Pop would have wrinkles like that one day. Wrinkles that held all his mistakes. I might not have been able to say it out loud, but I understood Old Red at that moment, and I liked him too.

"Jane, I haven't had a drink of liquor since that day. That was my bottom. And I carry that unloaded gun to remind me to stay sober."

My eyeballs became watery, and I quivered under the stiff white hospital sheets.

Old Red gently placed a spotted hand on my shoulder. "Young Jane, I know what you're thinking. Your pop can beat this too. I know he can."

I felt a tear trickle down my cheek. I didn't want Pop

to shoot anyone to make him finally stop drinking. I never wanted it to get that bad. I grabbed a tissue and wiped at my eyeballs. It was silent in that hospital room for a long spell, silent until my nose stopped running and my eyes dried a bit.

"I'm sorry about that little boy, Mr. Norton. Do you know what happened to him?"

Old Red nodded. "I do now," he said. "A few years back, I found out where he was living and that he wasn't doing too well. I've been keeping tabs on him."

"Wait." Something was beginning to make sense. Something about what Old Red mentioned at church a few days ago. "Is this boy the reason you are selling Three Boulders? Is he the person who's in trouble? Are you trying to help him?"

"You are smart as a whip, Jane Pengilly." He had a crooked, contented smile on his face, but he didn't say anything else. He closed his eyes.

I had way more questions to ask about the boy and Three Boulders and how Old Red was going to help, but I figured it was important to stop. A dude as ancient as Old Red needed his rest. Especially after sharing those secrets of his past.

By the time hippo ice cream man returned to take my temperature, Old Red was sawing some long raspy motor breaths. I just lay there and listened 'cause I liked the sound. It sounded an awful lot like Pop.

Day Eleven

A Hero's Welcome

There was an awesome policy in the hospital that all patients had to be escorted out in a wheelchair when they were released. I liked being pushed by hippo ice cream man. Today he was dolphin man, though, and he spun my chair in circles and even popped a few wheelies. I almost asked dolphin man to give me a ride to the third floor to the New Paradise Clinic, but I knew he couldn't do that. It was okay, though. Pop was going to get his story straight, and I was going to be back with him in just two days. I think knowing that Pop was so close to me in the hospital helped me heal faster.

My burned hand was doing so much better. The shooting red streaks were gone and so were the icky green goobers. It didn't hurt so much anymore either. Officer D came by in the morning and said that I had to take my antibiotics for five more days to keep fighting the infection.

I was happy to see G and Mrs. Biggs in the hospital lobby when dolphin man wheeled me out of the elevator. G had her arms around a stuffed raccoon and she skipped forward when she saw me and shoved the raccoon into my lap.

"Mom said I should buy you some flowers," G said, "but I saw this fuzzy guy in the gift shop and I thought you would like him more."

"Thanks, G." I gave the raccoon a squeeze. "I'll call him Boulder. That way when I see him, I'll always think about you and my twelve days in your weird little community."

G smiled, but it was a sad smile. Hippo ice cream dolphin man gave me a high five and told me to take care of my hand because as much as he liked me, he didn't want to see me back in the hospital.

We walked through the parking lot and loaded ourselves into Mrs. Biggs's sedan. G said that no one could stop talking about me in Three Boulders and what I had done for Timmy Spencer at the softball game.

I told G that Old Red had visited me yesterday, but I didn't say anything about him shooting the little boy. I had promised Old Red I could keep a secret, after all.

"Jane," G said softly, "Mr. Norton told us all at dinner last night that he found a buyer for his land." Her face was turned away from me, staring out the car window.

I wanted to tell her that everything was okay. She may have to leave Three Boulders, but she still had her mom and dad. I wanted to tell her that she would stay my friend. But I asked, "What about the money we're collecting? Once we add that all up, I'm sure we can make another offer to Mr. Norton."

Mrs. Biggs let out a whistle. "Yes, Gertie told us about your idea, Jane, to pool our money and buy the land." She scratched the super frizz on her head. "Folks in Three Boulders just don't have that kind of money."

Their pale faces were filled with sadness. But I knew how important it was for Old Red to have money so he could help that boy, who I realized was a grown man by now. I wanted to tell G and her mom that, but I wasn't the one who needed to explain. Only Old Red could do that.

We didn't say much more the rest of the trip. We rolled into the weedy Three Boulders parking lot, and G led the way up the path though all the fir trees and poky bushes. I followed her, holding on to my new raccoon, Boulder. When we reached the clearing to the gravel road, I heard a squeaking voice. It was Timmy Spencer.

"She's here!"

As I passed the last tree on the path, my eyeballs saw almost every human in Three Boulders gathered in a crowd. Loam Moonbeam and Mitchell Landau held up a long banner that read "The Mighty Catchers Thank You, Jane Pengilly." And everyone there was clapping with their hands high over their heads.

It was a hero's welcome, and I, Jane Pengilly, was the hero.

It made me think about a time when I was eight and Pop let me come with him to one of his meetings. He was getting a special coin for not drinking a single drop of alcohol for five hundred days straight. I was real proud of him, and I think Pop was proud too. Those folks at the meeting stood and clapped and cheered, and I even stood on one of the folding chairs and waved my hands above my head for him. Pop beamed his happy grin, and he walked to the front of the room for his shiny coin.

Right then, with the Three Boulders crowd cheering, I was feeling just the way Pop felt on his five hundred day.

But the thing was, I had just done what seemed right.

Timmy limped toward me. His ankle was taped up tight. He hugged me around my belly and asked if he could hold my raccoon. Then all those Three Boulders folks moved forward: Chef Noreen, Alan Stein, Mr. Biggs, Mama Amelia, the blondies, Preston Farmer, and every other Three Boulderite.

When Old Red stepped toward me, he shook my hand, strong and firm, just like Pop always taught me to do. He said to everyone, "Folks, we have a special dinner planned for tonight."

There was applause. I wondered what yumminess Chef Noreen would create.

"And," Old Red continued, "we'll be treating Jane to a Three Boulders talent show."

There was a smaller applause, mostly Dandy.

"Yes, I know it will be our final talent show," Old Red stated. "So let's make it our best. For Jane. For all of us."

The Talent Show

Chef Noreen made roasted chicken and fresh strawberry pie on a graham cracker crust for dessert. It was delicious and beyond. I was going to miss her cooking when I went back home to Pop.

I sat with G and her family. Timmy Spencer perched right next to me and he kept asking me questions about my burned hand and if he could see it without the bandages.

My brain didn't understand why Officer D wasn't here. I couldn't believe she would miss out on my celebration or on this pie. I asked Mr. Biggs where she was, but he didn't know. Then I asked Old Red, but he just told me that Officer D had lots of investigating to do tonight and she had to work late. I wondered why she couldn't do that investigating later.

There was a long twangy sound, and I looked up to see Alan Stein standing next to the fireplace blowing on a harmonica. He played us a song and rocked back and forth to his bluesy music. I drummed my hand on the table when he finished.

"Thank you. That was called 'Softball Game Blues,'" Mr. Stein said.

I bumped G in the shoulder because she wasn't clapping at all. "That was cool."

"He played the same song at our last talent show. He called it 'Springtime Blues' then," G answered.

"The same song?"

"Yes. The time before that it was called 'Blues for My Baby' and the time before that he called it 'Low-down Rotten Blues.' Mr. Stein only knows one song."

"Well, he plays it good."

Mr. Stein continued. "Good evening to all the folks of Three Boulders and especially our guest of honor, Miss Jane Pengilly."

My ears soaked in all the clapping.

"And now, let's continue this talent show by welcoming Miss Megan Donald."

Blondie Megan walked to the fireplace and sang the national anthem with no extra music, just her voice. Everyone rose. Pop and me agreed that this song was way too long, and we always wondered what ramparts were. Maybe I'd have to ask Old Red. He'd probably know.

After the clapping for Megan died off, Loam, Mitchell, and the Stein kid moved to the front of the dining hall and did a skit about a bus stop and a bench in which absolutely nothing happened, but they were cracking each other up. G had a grin on her face the whole time. It was the happiest she had looked all evening.

When the skit ended, Mitchell and the Stein kid sat down on the benches, but Loam stayed at the fireplace. He waved his hand and Dandy joined him. Loam cleared his throat and announced, "Dandy and I have a confession to make."

G's eyeballs bulged. She grabbed my good arm. The Three Boulders crowd hushed, waiting, watching Loam and Dandy. Mr. and Mrs. Moonbeam glanced at each other.

"We actually want to explain something. Something about the Three Boulders vortex," Loam said.

Dandy clapped her hands.

"You see, the vortex doesn't really exist." Loam scratched at his messy hair. "Dandy and I *are* the vortex. Everything you've lost, we have."

He walked to the front door of the dining hall where a large suitcase sat. He lugged the suitcase back to the fireplace, laid it down flat, and opened it slowly and carefully so nothing would fall out.

"This isn't all of it. We still have more, but we'll return it all, we promise."

Loam's voice cracked. Dandy stopped clapping. The Three Boulders crowd became a room of statues. No one moved. Not an inch. But me and G were smiling, especially me.

"Oh, Loam." It was Mrs. Moonbeam who finally spoke.

"I'm sorry, Mom. Dandy is too. We're stopping. We are done stealing things. For real. We promise."

"I believe you, Loam," I said, walking straight up to the fireplace next to dirt boy. I was proud of him. Telling the truth was hard sometimes. I knew that. But Loam was doing the right thing. It was his first step toward shaking his ogre.

"I'll help you return those vortex treasures," I announced.

"Me too," G said, marching up to the fireplace.

We all reached into the suitcase. Dandy pulled out purple gloves and took them to Millie Donald. G grabbed a yellow candle and handed it to Mrs. Carter. I didn't know who to give stuff to, but Loam told me. One colored item at a time, we delivered the sucked-away things that once formed Dandy's rainbow masterpiece.

"We know we can't apologize enough," Loam said when we finished, "but I want to show you what we did with everything. What Dandy did." He held up a photograph of the bookshelf in their closet. Dandy held up a piece of paper with a rainbow she had drawn. "Pass these around."

I watched, and I could tell by the way their jaws moved and their eyes glowed, that every person who saw that photo was as amazed as me and G had been just a few days earlier. Mrs. Moonbeam threw them kisses into the air.

Then Old Red thumped his shotgun cane one time and got everyone's attention. "Loam and Dandy, your confession is appreciated." He scanned all the pleased faces of the folks holding their long-lost possessions. "Shall we continue our celebration? I believe we have more talent to showcase, don't we, Alan?"

"Indeed we do." Mr. Stein rose and announced, "Next up on the Three Boulders stage is Miss Gertrude Biggs."

Was I ever surprised to hear that name. "G! You didn't tell me you would be in this show."

G walked cautiously toward the fireplace with her backpack. She reached into her pack and pulled out a thin felt bag. Her hands shook.

I quickly looked around for Officer D, but she *still* wasn't back from Willis.

From the felt bag, G slid out a smooth, black recorder. It was just like the recorders I learned to play in third grade, and I held in a groan because those recorders were harsh on the ears. My music teacher always told me I blew too loud, and usually she took my recorder away from me.

But G began to blow, and the sound that came from her stick was not the shrill recorder-snatching sound I was expecting. She didn't play "Hot Cross Buns" or "Pop Goes the Weasel." She played a song I'd never heard before. It was comforting like Noreen's mac and cheese, but with a dash of that red pepper to give it zest. The whole audience became silent. Our eyeballs locked on G. Our ears soaked up her notes.

G was . . . well, G was awesome. It was the best I had ever heard that little squawk stick played.

When she finished, I stood up and stepped on the bench and hollered, "Woo-hoo, G!"

The applause was huge, the biggest of the night so far. Mrs. Biggs had tears in her eyes and so did Chef Noreen.

Every member of the sunshine gang stood and lifted their hands over their heads to clap for G.

G bowed, then slid her recorder back into the felt bag, scooped up her backpack, and walked toward me.

"You rocked the dining hall down, G! How'd you learn to do that?"

She beamed. "Thanks. I taught myself. It's kind of my secret."

"What was that song called?"

"It's something I wrote that reminds me of you. I'm calling it 'When Jane Came to Three Boulders.'"

My brain went blank. It couldn't find words to send to my mouth.

Not one.

Not even a gulp or a peep.

I think that concerned G because she asked, "Jane, did you like it? It's kind of an early going-away present for you."

I still couldn't talk.

All I could do was nod my head because I did like G's song. I really, *really* liked it.

I think I couldn't talk because my brain was attempting to sort out thoughts and feelings from this night and my other days in Three Boulders that I'd never had to sort before. It was like a bunch of socks had been tossed in my brain drawer, and none of them were matching. The drawer was a mixture of sock colors and sizes. I needed the blue right sock to go with the blue left sock and the right-smiley face sock to go with the left-smiley face sock because that had always worked for me . . . two socks made a pair, like me and Pop. There were suddenly so many socks in my drawer, but I couldn't find any pairs.

I didn't understand why there was so much messiness in my brain.

Day Twelve

What Social Services Fran Thought

On the last day of Pop's rehab, my hand was barely even aching, just a teeny-weeny little throb, and only when I pushed on it. My brain felt better too after all that muddled confusion from the night before. These had to be good signs, signs that everything was going to be okay with me and Pop. I couldn't wait to see him.

I hummed one of Pop's silly songs as I began grabbing some of my shorts and T-shirts that I had shoved under Officer D's couch. I was folding up my black hoodie when there was a knock on the door. It was G.

"Hi, Jane. I was going to go practice my recorder before breakfast. Do you want to come?"

Half of me wanted to go with G more than anything, even more than eating three or four of Noreen's sticky doughnuts. But the other half of me remembered how I felt last night when I heard her play, that sock drawer confusion.

I didn't actually have to decide because there was a second knock at the door, and Officer D let in Old Red.

"Good morning," he said to all of us and made himself at home in the stiff chair next to my lumpy sleeping couch. He wasn't carrying his shotgun.

"Gertie, I'd like you to head downstairs. Mr. Norton and I need to have a confidential conversation with Jane." Officer D wore her serious cop face.

G moved toward the door, but I grabbed her arm. "G can stay."

Officer D and Old Red exchanged lingering glances. Officer D frowned. "Fine. Sit on the couch, girls."

I tossed some clothes over to one side. G sat on the end, near the chair where Old Red was, and I perched in the lumpy middle. Officer D scooped up a folding chair by her bed and propped it open directly in front of me. She sat her burly self down with her spine all tall and straight.

Officer D's face changed to her worried look, so I said, "You don't have to worry about my hand anymore, you know."

"I'm not worried about your hand, Jane." She pressed her lips together and rubbed her palms. She was having a hard time getting words out right now, kind of like me last night when I felt all confused about G and Three Boulders.

And then I figured it out.

Officer D was sad about me leaving tomorrow. And she

didn't have a squawky recorder to play to tell me how she felt.

"Officer D," I said, helping her out, "you've been a real great foster person to me these last twelve days, my favorite foster person yet—"

"Oh, Jane. I . . ." She stared at me intently. Old Red stared at me too. I didn't like those looks. I didn't like them at all.

"Jane, I need to give you some news about your pop," Officer D said.

I felt a little warning zap in my head. "Is Pop sick?"

She let out a huge sigh. "He's not sick. It's just that there's been—"

"Did he do something wrong?"

Officer D shook her head. "That's not it. He's doing fine with his rehab, following all the rules like always."

"Then what's wrong?" My stomach was queasy now, but not from hunger and not from my infected burn like a few days ago. Something was wrong, and all the parts inside my chest could feel it. It was like all those little inner cells of mine were kicking and screaming.

Officer D dropped her head, looking at her legs. She kept rubbing her hands, forward and back, forward and back. I think everyone in the room could feel the heat she was making in her palms.

"Doris, tell her," Old Red said.

Officer D sucked in a long breath. "Jane, yesterday I spoke with Fran. After you were admitted to the hospital with the infection, she became more concerned. She insisted she needed more time to investigate the night your hand was burned so badly. She won't let you return to your pop until she is *certain* of what happened that night. She needs to believe what both of you have said."

Officer D's words shoved me into the back of the couch.

What?

I can't go back to Pop?

Memories of that night swirled in my brain, the red coils on the stove top, Pop real deep asleep, lying in the living room.

I had told Pop *exactly* what to say. He was supposed to say he was resting. He heard me start dinner. We danced. I slipped and burned my hand on the stove. He called 911. End of story.

Why didn't they believe him?

Did Pop say something different?

"What . . . what do you mean?" I asked instead, reining in those other questions.

"Fran doesn't think your father is telling the truth." Officer D paused. "She doesn't think the burn on your hand was an accident." Her voice was quieter and softer than ever. She reached her man paw for my good hand and squeezed it.

So Pop *had* told them it was an accident. He told them exactly what I had told them.

There shouldn't be a problem.

I squirmed a bit on the lumpy couch cushions. I could feel three sets of eyeballs on me.

There was no way that flame-shoed Fran could know what really happened that night.

I tried to think back to the emergency room, sitting on the crinkly white paper on the examining table. Fran had asked me so many questions: Was Pop good to me? Did he ever hurt me? Did I ever feel afraid with him?

And I had answered her questions.

Yes. No. No.

Those were my forever answers.

"Young Jane," Old Red said, "sometimes when a person has been drinking, he does things that he wouldn't normally do. Sometimes he may not even remember doing those things."

I glared at Old Red and swallowed a big gulp of air. "What does she think happened?"

The room went dead quiet. Old Red leaned back. G's bottom lip quivered. Officer D lifted my hand and pressed it to her cheek, but I pulled it away.

"Wait." My inner cells were in a full-out war now. "She thinks Pop did this?" I held up my burned hand. "She thinks he hurt me?"

Officer D put both her hands on my shoulders now. "I don't know exactly what she thinks, Jane."

I twisted away from her and stood up. "It isn't true!" I hollered. "Pop didn't hurt me! He would never, *ever* hurt me!"

I was stomping my feet hard as I said those words, and I didn't care if all the Three Boulders folks in the dining hall below could hear me.

"Officer D, you go tell that social services Fran that Pop didn't hurt me!"

Officer D shook her head. "Jane, we have to be thorough in our investigation. We have to follow the law."

"What law? What are you talking about?" I stomped my foot again. "When can I go back to Pop?"

Officer D looked at Old Red. "Jane, please sit back down." She was almost whispering now. "It's possible . . ." She hesitated, glancing at Old Red again. "It's possible your pop will be arrested."

The room went stony silent, silent enough to hear an eyelid blink. And it stayed that way for what felt like a lifetime, my whole lifetime with Pop.

I remembered the way he twirled me over his head when I was real little and I giggled so much I drooled on his forehead. I remembered longboarding times, bombing the big hills and chillin' down the gentle slopes. I remembered watching all the dumb reality shows, eating popcorn together.

Arrested?

Did she really say that?

I gripped my head with both hands and squeezed hard. It felt like my sock drawer brain had been flung open. The Pop socks flew one way. The Jane socks flew the other way. I squeezed tighter and tighter and tighter.

I inhaled a shaky gulp of air.

I'd been holding in the truth for twelve days, keeping it secret from everyone.

I kept squeezing and squeezing my head, holding in that sock explosion.

I didn't want Pop to get arrested. I had to tell the truth. I might get in trouble, and Pop might be really mad at me, but the honest truth might be the only thing that could save Pop—save us.

I felt tears making a path down both my cheeks, and I looked into Officer D's eyes. "I lied," I whispered. "I lied about my hand. It wasn't an accident."

Confessions

G gasped. Old Red leaned forward. Officer D grabbed my shoulders again and gripped hard. "Oh, Jane. What happened?"

My nose started dripping alongside my tears. I was shuddering now, and Officer D pulled me into her beefy chest. Old Red rose from the chair and handed me a handkerchief. I gave a big blubbering blow and shook some more.

I let the honest words gush from my mouth. "You know Pop, Officer D. You know that he's a good person. It's just that this time, he was *real* bad off. I don't know why. I think his sadness was just too much. We were having lots of bad me-and-Pop days."

I took a deep, shaky breath. "He was still walking me to school, and he still went to the warehouse to work, but he drank his yucky alcohol every night instead of coffee. He was falling asleep on the couch. He wasn't talking to me much. I was really lonely, and I missed him bad."

I stopped and rubbed the tears from my cheek. "I had to help him. He needed to go to rehab."

G reached for my hand. For just a teeny moment, I wished I was Gertrude Biggs, a girl who had lived most her life in the safety of Three Boulders with all the nice people around her every day, and all the weird laws that everyone followed . . . mostly. But then I was mad at myself for thinking that, for thinking of a life without Pop. I loved Pop.

"Jane, what happened that night?" Officer D asked again.

I sucked in another trembly breath. "Pop fell asleep on the couch, facedown, and I couldn't wake him up. I shook him as hard as I could. I yelled at him. I threw pillows at him. I wanted to throw that stupid bottle at him, but I didn't. Nothing I did made him budge. He just lay there like he was dead, but he wasn't dead because I checked. I know how to check for a pulse." My voice and shoulders shuddered. "I had to get him to wake up, and I realized there was only one way to do it."

"How?" G whispered.

I wondered what G was thinking of me right then and whether she was still going to be my friend when she knew the truth.

I honked my nose into Old Red's handkerchief again. "I used to have nightmares when I was little. Pop said they were just bad ogres trapped in my brain, but I'd wake up screaming the strands of hair off my head.

"One time when we lived in Walport, a neighbor heard me. I was *that* loud. Pop *always* heard my screams. It never mattered how much he may have drank." I tossed Old Red's hankie on the floor 'cause it was a goobery mess. Officer D didn't seem to care. She just grabbed a box of tissues from the table next to the couch and handed them to me.

"So that night," I continued, "I sat on the floor next to the couch, and I screamed and shrieked just like when those ogres invaded my brain, but Pop didn't wake up, so I screamed more. I even banged my fist on the wall. Then I realized that maybe he didn't wake up because I was faking it. I can't bluff Pop with nothing."

Officer D slowly shook her head. She rested her man paws on my knees. "Oh, Jane," she whispered.

"So that's when I came up with the idea of making my screams real. It was the only way. I had to think of a way to hurt myself bad enough to let out my night ogre shrieks." My voice was cracking. I wasn't sounding like me at all, but it was me. It was my voice finally telling the honest truth.

"So . . . I went to the kitchen and turned on the stove. I waited until those coils got toasty red, and I—"

"Stop!" G yelled. "Please stop!"

G started sobbing, and Old Red scooted forward in the stiff chair and rubbed her back, but he was looking at me, gazing into my eyeballs with the kindest look I'd seen from him in twelve days.

G lowered her face into her lap, and I knew that my new friend didn't need to hear any more of this story, so I stopped my gush of words. G was smart. She could figure it out.

"Why didn't you just call nine-one-one?" Officer D asked, her eyeballs watery. "You didn't have to do this to yourself." She touched my wrist. "If you had called, I would have helped get your pop to rehab."

"I tried, Officer D, but Pop's phone was in his front pocket. He was lying on top of it. I couldn't get it out. He was too heavy to turn over."

Officer D rubbed her watery eyes, and I tried explaining some more. "Even if I had called you, I don't know if Pop would have gone to rehab. He always told me that no one can really heal unless he wants to heal. No one could make him go to rehab except himself."

I kept peering at Officer D, trying to make her understand. "When Pop heard my real scream, he *did* wake up. He saw how hurt I was. *He* called nine-one-one and *he* volunteered to go right to rehab." I pulled in some trembling breaths, and then said softly, "I saved him."

Officer D closed her eyelids tight, which squeezed out some tears. They dribbled down the sides of her face.

"So you see, you can't let Pop be arrested. He didn't do anything wrong, and we should be able to be together. I promise I won't hurt myself again. I promise."

Officer D let her tears drip right onto the stiffness of her navy-blue cop collar.

"Jane, don't you see that this isn't healthy?"

I held up my bandaged hand. "This?" I said. "My hand is doing fine."

"I'm not talking about your hand, Jane." Her voice was louder now. "I'm talking about you and your pop. You're not a healthy family."

"What . . . what do you mean?"

My deepest and worst fear in the universe crept into my gut. Even after spilling the whole truth, I was still losing Pop. They were going to take Pop away from me. I felt kind of numb. I could hardly even wiggle my fingers.

"Jane." She glanced at Old Red, like she was expecting him to say something. Then she peered into my eyes. "I'm moving into an apartment in Willis. It's in the same building as Mr. Norton's new apartment." She paused. "I'd like you to live with me. I'll take care of you." She looked at Old Red again. "*We'll* take care of you. We'd both like that—very much."

I stared at Officer D's face real close. It wasn't her serious cop face or her questioning face or her worried face, the three faces I knew so well. Her green eyes were a little blurry and her nostrils flared just a bit, and nothing but kindness gushed from her cheeks. She was the best foster person I'd ever lived with—the best foster *mom*.

But . . . didn't she know that Pop needed me?

Didn't she know that I needed . . .

I needed . . .

I shook my head. "I like you a lot, Officer D . . . and you too, Mr. Norton, but I'm supposed to be with family, right? That's what Pop says. He's the only family I have."

G lifted her face and put her arm around me. I rested my head on her shoulder, and I felt this small moment of warmth, like G had pulled a fuzzy towel from a hot dryer and wrapped it around me. We sat like that for a while.

Then Old Red scooted forward in the chair and said, "Actually, young Jane, that's not true. You do have more family."

I lifted my head off G's shoulder and Old Red and me had a sudden staring contest. I studied each and every wrinkle and warty spot on his ancient face. My eyeballs weren't budging.

He blinked first, losing our staring contest. He scratched behind his mug-handle ears. "Jane, I know what I'm going to say will be a shock to you, but you *have* family. Right here in Three Boulders." He paused, a long, clock-ticking pause.

"You have a great-grandfather."

What was he talking about?

I did *not* have a great-grandfather.

My family was Pop. Only Pop. If Old Red had looked at G's journal entry about me, he would know that.

I kept staring at Old Red. I still hadn't blinked.

"It's me, Jane. Old Red." He cleared his throat. "Your great-grandfather."

Redemption

Now what in the universe was a kid supposed to say when a shotgun-toting, wrinkly ancient dude confessed that he was your great-grandfather? Was I supposed to fling my arms around him and hug him? Was I supposed to act all relieved that I suddenly had another blood relative that I never knew existed? Why didn't he just tell me he was my great-grandfather when we first met? Why didn't Officer D tell me?

Why didn't *Pop* tell me?

It was impossible to understand how I kept all these questions from spewing out of my mouth. But for some reason, I did. Maybe it was because this announcement was so incredibly big. It was a giant snake, squeezing my vocal cords, not allowing a single peep to be released.

So I did the only other thing I was capable of doing at that moment.

I bolted.

I shot off the couch past Old Red. I slammed Officer D's door behind me and tore down the stairs and through the dining hall. Heads turned. I heard Timmy Spencer say "Hi, Jane!" but I kept running, out the doors of the dining hall and then up the gravel road. My shoes filled with tiny stones, and they wedged themselves through the holes in my socks and poked the skin around my toes, but I didn't stop running. I ran up the hill, past all the tidy log cabins, through the fir-lined path, into the grassy clearing toward the three boulders. And when I got there, the bright morning sun was beaming on the rocks. They almost looked red in the sunlight, like giant, protective garnets.

I stepped onto Tortoise Back and slumped down in exhaustion. The rock was warm against the skin on my calves.

I thought about Pop and me and our house in Willis. I squeezed tears away wondering when I would see him again.

I thought about Officer D and that mom face and how she wanted me to stay with her.

I thought about my new best friend, G, and her special recorder song.

I thought about Loam and Dandy and their secret rainbow, and little Timmy Spencer, the pint-size Babe Ruth.

I thought about Old Red and his shotgun story and his

claim that he was my great-grandfather.

I thought about this crazy little community of Three Boulders that would be gone very soon: the garden, Noreen's dining hall, the softball game, record night, the laws, the fire pit with the pew logs, the talent show, the nicest folks ever.

I was thinking so much that I had no idea how long I had been there, and I didn't even notice when G climbed onto the boulder and sat down next to me. She opened her backpack and pulled out a blueberry muffin wrapped in a napkin and set it on my legs. She handed me a bottle of orange juice and some shoestring turnip slices. I ate everything.

"How'd you know I was here?"

G shrugged. "I just knew."

I slugged down the last drops of orange juice, and G spoke again. "I think you are the bravest person in the world, Jane Pengilly."

I didn't feel brave right now.

"You mean the stupidest?"

"No," G answered. "You were trying to help your pop. The whole way up here, I tried to figure out if I could ever do something like that, risk myself for another person in my family. Loam did it too. He risked himself for Dandy, but I just don't know if I could. I'm not as strong as you, Jane. I'm mostly scared." She turned her head away from me. "I'm

terrified of leaving Three Boulders." She ran her pointy finger down the side of Steel Marble.

"Everyone is scared of something, G."

And I knew that was the truth. I was scared of losing
Pop. Pop was scared of losing me. Loam was scared of losing
Dandy. Even Old Red Norton was scared. I think he was
scared of me, scared to tell me the honest truth when he
first met me.

I stood up on the flat boulder that I called Tortoise Back
and put my hand on the Majestic Spire, feeling the grooves
in the rock.

"Redemption," G said. "It means 'the act of setting free,
or making up for, or saving from sin.'"

I tossed that definition around—setting free—making
up for—saving from sin. I think Pop needed redemption
a lot. That's why he went to rehab. I thought that burning
my hand would save him and set us both free, but it didn't.
Burning my hand was wrong. Maybe it was a sin.

Maybe *I* needed redemption.

G dusted the crumbs off her skirt. "I talked to Loam a
few minutes ago. He told me what he saw in that old blue
People of Three Boulders journal, the one he wanted us to
look at the other day."

I stared at G.

"There was an entry for your pop, Jerry Pengilly. He

lived in Three Boulders when he was seven. It mentioned that Old Red was his grandfather. That's what Loam wanted to tell you."

I couldn't sort this all out. Why didn't Pop ever tell me that? He said there was only us. Pop and Jane.

But that wasn't true. We did have more family.

"My brain aches, G," I said, clamping my hands over my stocking cap.

G rubbed my back, and we sat quiet together.

"Guess what?" she asked after a bit. "I've brought camping gear for us. Officer Dashell and my mom and dad said that you and I could spend the night right up here at the boulders."

She jumped off Community boulder and picked up a bag. "I brought a tent."

"We're going to camp on the boulders?" I asked.

"Not on *top* of the boulders," she said. "We could set up the tent over there." She pointed to a small area of dirt and pine needles.

Me and Pop lived at the Lizard Creek Campground once for four weeks while he searched for a job. It was my least favorite home ever. I didn't like the ants that crawled on me inside the tent, or how our hot dogs got charred in the fire, or how my sleeping bag was damp in the morning. The only thing I did like was snuggling next to Pop, staring at our lantern, and watching the bugs in the halo of light while he told me stories.

"My dad is bringing sleeping bags and food for us later. It'll be fun. I brought my recorder to play and some of my favorite books."

G's usual pale face had a little tinge of pink. Even her frizzy hair looked tame. At the moment, she didn't look scared of anything, and that made me smile on the inside.

There was no way I was ready to face Officer D and certainly not Old Red, so maybe camping with G would be okay. Maybe she would play that song again for me on her recorder, or something else she had written. Maybe I could forget about Pop for just a little bit . . . maybe.

For some reason, I glanced at her unzipped backpack. I saw the tip of her recorder bag poking out and two or three books, but nothing else. "G, where are all your journals?"

"I gave them to Old Red last night, right after the talent show. I realized he should be the one to have them. This is his community. He needs to keep all those memories when he leaves."

I looked at G again. G without those journals she loved so much.

I filled up with a whole gallon of pride for her right then. Handing over those journals was like G's way of letting go and moving forward. She was setting herself free.

That was G's redemption.

The Next Day

The Rest of the Story

A squawking bird woke me in the morning. I had slept horribly on my earth mattress. Too many little rocks had poked into my back, and my brain couldn't stop thinking of Pop. He was probably packing his bags at the New Paradise Clinic, expecting to see my face when he came into the lobby, ready to take me home, make a box or three of mac and cheese, and watch some TV with me right at his side. But now that probably wouldn't happen. Now he might be greeted by social services Fran and a cop with handcuffs. I shook that thought away as fast as I could.

I rolled over and discovered G's sleeping bag was empty. There was a note on her pillow: *Hi, Jane. I went down to the dining hall to get us some breakfast. Don't go anywhere. Love, G.*

I was a little sweaty inside my sleeping bag. The morning sun beamed into the tent from the open gap near the top. I stretched my arms and legs, pulled on Pop's orange stocking cap, and unzipped the door.

Resting on top of the Community boulder was Old Red Norton. There was a big crooked stick leaning against the Forgiveness boulder. I wondered how long it had taken him to trek up the hill from his cabin. He turned when he heard the zipping and nodded at me. I wanted to zip the door up and crawl back inside, pretending I hadn't seen him, but I had to pee something fierce.

I slipped on my shoes and walked toward the little grove of trees that G and I decided would be our outhouse. I made sure I was well hidden from Old Red before I did my business.

As I walked back toward the tent, he spoke calmly, "I imagine you have a lot to say to me."

He sure had that right. Angry words gushed from my mouth. "I'm not real happy with you for keeping a secret like you did. You should have just told me the truth the first time we met. You watched me with your hawk eyeballs all week. You listened to me tell what I did to my hand, and then when it looks like I can't go home to Pop, you blurt out that you're my great-grandfather. You should have told me before!"

There, I said it. My cheeks were heated up, and my fists were clenched in balls, but I felt a wee bit better.

"If I had told you when we met on your first day in Three Boulders, would you have believed me?"

"How am I supposed to know that?"

"You get brought to a strange place by a cop, thinking you would stay for twelve days, and the first person you see is an old geezer in a rocking chair who tells you he is your great-grandfather. Would you have believed me?"

I kicked my shoes into the dirt, popping up little stones. "No."

Old Red let out a big exhale. "That's what I thought." He shifted on the boulder, moving closer to his crooked stick. "Sit down, Jane."

"No, thank you."

But Old Red gave me a shotgun-raising look, enhancing those wrinkles around his nose, and I moved to the boulder, sitting as far from him as I possibly could, my back to his side.

"I didn't finish my whole story the other day in the hospital. I have more to tell you."

I peeked over my shoulder. Old Red grasped his crooked stick and perched it between his legs. "I've mentioned my daughter, Florence, and how you remind me of her. Florence loved Three Boulders as a child, just like I'd hoped. As she grew older though, she wanted to move on, to see what the world beyond this little haven had to offer. She left to find a new life." Old Red made a soft snoring sound as he inhaled a new breath of air.

"Florence sent me letters telling me of her life, how she

had finished college and worked as a journalist, how she had met a wonderful man named Clark Pengilly, and they had married on the coast, barefoot in the sand."

My brain clicked and recognized that Florence was *my* grandmother, and I found myself turning toward Old Red, inching closer to him to hear his words better. I wished I could see a picture of my grandmother, standing in the sand. I wondered if she was skinny like me and Pop, and Old Red, and whether her hair was stick straight like mine.

"And then she sent the wonderful news that she had a son, a son she named Jeremiah. It warmed my heart knowing that I had a grandson. I ached to meet him and to see Florence again, so I invited them all to return to Three Boulders."

Old Red looked older all of a sudden, if that's even possible.

I finally spoke. "And they came. I know that Pop lived in Three Boulders."

"Did he tell you that?" Old Red asked.

I shook my head. "No." But I didn't explain how I knew. "How long did he live here?"

"Sadly for me, not very long. Perhaps two years."

"Why'd they leave?" I was completely facing him now, sitting crisscross applesauce on the boulder.

"They left because of me. Because of my actions." His

shoulders slumped forward. A pain in his heart seemed to be pulling on him. He gripped his crooked stick tighter. "Jane, the little boy I shot in the leg that one night, thinking it was a mountain lion, was my grandson. He was your pop."

I gasped. My hands covered my face.

Stuff inside my brain started to make sense. I thought of Pop getting shot when he was so little. That must have been awful. I thought of all those scars on his leg and how he told me he was attacked by a blackberry bush.

"Pop lied to me," I whispered.

Old Red sighed. "Young Jane, your pop was probably trying to protect you. He probably thought you would be scared to learn he had been shot by his own grandfather."

But I wasn't so sure. There was so much Pop kept from me. So much about my family.

My brain felt all scrambled and messy again. I yanked on Pop's stocking cap.

Old Red reached into his chest pocket and pulled out three pictures, handing them to me. They were the thick photos with white borders, and I gazed at a little boy, maybe six years old, sitting on top of a blue bicycle. The second one was of that same boy in a tree and a woman was reaching up to him, and then the third photo with that same woman, younger in this shot, sitting on the dining hall steps. My pop and my grandma.

"You may keep those," Old Red said.

"No way." I quickly tucked the pictures back in his shirt pocket. "I can't do that. They are your good memories."

Old Red smiled, and it almost seemed like a few of his wrinkles ironed away at that moment.

"How did you find out about me?"

He lifted his eyebrows a bit. "That's a fair question. Many people have come in and out of Three Boulders, and many stay in contact with me. Your grandmother's good friend, Helen, drove from Idaho to see me after she heard that Florence had passed.

"And, of course, Officer Dashell used her connections to keep tabs on you and your pop for quite a few years. I asked her to. I was pleased when she informed me that you two had moved to Willis, just a short drive down the highway."

Stuff was making more sense. All Officer D's visits to our house over the last year. All the times she and Pop would stand in the driveway and talk while I watched from the kitchen window. They weren't just talking about everyday, ordinary stuff like I figured. They were probably talking about Old Red and Three Boulders.

Old Red began to chuckle from his belly. "Doris told me you were a pistol, Jane. She took a strong liking to you. She told me stories of you and your pop longboarding in the park after curfew and having to send you both home."

Those were good me-and-Pop times. Pop always said that longboarding at midnight under the streetlights was his favorite.

"Doris called me, right after you were taken to the hospital with your burn. She said she could do some paperwork and that she could bring you to Three Boulders while your pop was in rehab. I can't tell you how happy that made me."

I was sitting close enough to Old Red now that I could feel his arm brush against mine. I could smell just a whiff of aftershave too, the same kind Pop uses. "Mr. Norton," I began, because questions and facts were organizing in my brain. "The money you get for selling Three Boulders. Is that money for Pop?"

"For you and your pop," he answered. "I can't live up here any longer knowing how much you're both struggling. I want your pop to recover, to have more therapy if he needs it. I don't want you hopping from place to place between each relapse and job. I want *you* to be safe and happy." He looked me straight in the eyeballs. "Officer Dashell wants you safe too. She cares for you deeply, Jane. So do I."

I almost flung my arms around Old Red's skinny chest. I almost told him that I cared about him too, but I didn't do those things because there was something I still didn't understand, something that kind of prickled at my heart.

I cleared my throat and asked carefully, "Why didn't you ever try to come see me and Pop yourself?"

Old Red lifted his eyes to the sky, like he was listening to words from God, swirling over our heads. His voice quivered when he spoke. "Young Jane, that is a deep regret of mine. You see, I wasn't sure if I'd be welcome. There is so much sorrow in the past." He turned his head and gazed directly at Redemption.

I'd never had a teacher tell me that I'm smart. Oh sure, they've told me that I *exert effort* or that I have *unique gifts*, but they never say I'm smart. Right then, though, sitting on the Community boulder with Old Red, I *felt* supersmart, because I had figured something out.

Old Red had been a drinker. He had done some bad things. He had left his orchard in California. He had stolen money from his brother. He had shot his own grandson . . . by accident, of course.

I had it all figured out.

Old Red needed redemption too.

And then I glanced at the round boulder I called Steel Marble but which Old Red named Forgiveness.

I realized that to have redemption, you had to have forgiveness.

Old Red was living up here in Three Boulders, almost hiding away, because he hadn't forgiven himself.

He hadn't forgiven himself for anything.

Matching Socks

There was only one thing in the whole universe that would have made me leave Old Red sitting there by himself on the Community boulder after telling me his story.

And that one thing—well, person, really—was moving toward me through the grassy clearing.

Pop.

I blinked my eyes hard to be sure I wasn't imagining him, but it was really him. Pop with his black stocking cap resting just above his ears. Pop with his dusky orange T-shirt with the fading words The Clash. Pop with a fish-shaped longboard propped over his shoulder.

I leaped off the boulder and flung myself at him, squeezing his belly and burying my head in his warm, sweaty chest. He wrapped his arms across my back, dropping the longboard at our feet, and then he scooped under my armpits and lifted me in the air, tossing me above his head like I was still three years old.

When he set me down, I still felt like I was flying in the air with happiness. I hugged him again. "Pop! Are you okay? Are you dry again? I was worried about you."

"Dry as a camel's mouth in the desert, Jane Girl." He winked at me, and just as he did, it registered in my brain that he wasn't alone. He had brought a crowd. There was Officer D; my best friend, G; Mr. and Mrs. Biggs; Timmy Spencer and his mama, Amelia; the Donalds; the Carters; Preston Farmer; Chef Noreen; and even Loam and Dandy.

"What's going on?" I let go of Pop's waist and grabbed his hand. I looked over at Officer D. "Pop wasn't arrested?"

She stepped forward. "Jane, I had a talk with Fran. I told her the story about your . . . incident."

I glanced at Pop when she said that, and his eyeballs gave me a serious look that I understood without any words. He had been told what I had done, and he never wanted me to do it again. He didn't need to worry. I had no plans to ever hurt myself again. I did a silent cross-my-heart-hope-to-die-stick-a-needle-in-my-eye promise.

"They are allowing you to return to your father, but with some strict guidelines," Officer D continued.

"What guidelines?" I asked.

"To begin, there will be twice-weekly home visits and interviews with each of you."

Officer D was speaking slowly, like something was wedged in her throat that made it hard to push out the words.

"And," she went on, "your pop will be required to attend daily meetings, twice a day at first, and have no unreasonable absences from work."

"Jane," Pop said. He pulled the orange stocking cap off my head and ruffled my hair. "I have my job back at the warehouse, forty hours a week beginning Monday. We'll stay in Willis. We don't have to move."

That all should have been good news to me. Sometimes after Pop got out of rehab, it took him months to find a new job. But I didn't know what was wrong inside my brain because the news wasn't setting off much excitement.

I looked back at Officer D. She was staring at the brown pine needles under her feet.

"We survived another twelve days," Pop said. "We can go home now. You and me. Matching socks."

That was the honest truth. I had survived the twelve days. Twelve days in Three Boulders. And in those twelve days, I had met Gertie Biggs, and we went to school and church together, and we snuck off to Willis, and she wrote a special song for me.

I peered at Officer D, my foster per— my foster *mom*, and I thought of the twelve days I stayed in her little room above the dining hall, and how she changed my bandage, and how she put her strong man paw on my head each morning to wake me, and how she ran with me in her arms all the way to her truck to get me to the hospital.

I scanned the other faces lined up before me: little twitchy, home-run-hitting Timmy Spencer; klepto dirt-boy Loam; rainbow weed-girl Dandy; Chef Noreen. And I remembered more stuff from those twelve days, the school that wasn't really like school, the church service where God spoke to us in the wind, the softball game that made me a town hero, the talent show where G displayed her brilliance on the squawk stick, the yummy food Noreen cooked for us every day, the rainbow masterpiece that Dandy built . . .

I looked over my shoulder. Old Red still sat on the Community boulder, holding his crooked walking cane. He hadn't moved a muscle.

Old Red.

My great-grandfather.

My . . . Old Pop.

Pop took hold of my shoulders and pulled me in for another hug. "Are you packed?"

I stepped back, releasing his arms, and I gave Pop my best serious, Officer D–like look. "No," I said.

"Well, come on, then." He softly punched my good arm. "Let's get moving. We've got some hills to bomb in Willis." He reached down and grabbed his new board.

Looking at Pop right at that moment, I thought about

how much I loved him, and that really required about a hundred or more thoughts because I loved my pop a lot. A whole lot.

But what I said to him was, "No, Pop."

He lifted an eyebrow. "Jane?"

"Pop," I began, but I had to stop and swallow. There was some reorganizing happening in my sock drawer. More sock pairs were being rolled together, pairs for me and G, me and Officer D, me and Old Red, and me and all the other really nice folks of Three Boulders. Those pairs tucked themselves into my drawer, like cushions around the Pop and Jane socks.

I gazed at Pop and said, "I don't want to go back to Willis or any other town. I want to stay in Three Boulders."

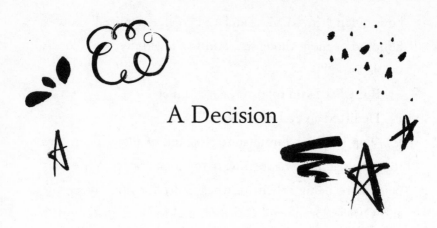

A Decision

I think it's possible to know that things are happening even if you don't really see them with your own eyes. Right then, when I said those words, I was staring at Pop's face, but I'm pretty sure that G and Officer D and maybe everyone else had their mouths dropped open and their eyes locked on me.

"I don't understand." Pop tugged on my stocking cap. "We got this, Jane Girl."

Here was Pop in front of me, dry, happy, ready to move on with our lives like we had done many times before.

Pop and me.

Me and Pop.

I spoke softly. "No, I don't think we got this anymore."

I gulped in a burst of boonieville air and continued. "This place, Three Boulders, is the weirdest place I've ever been, Pop, but I really like it."

I snuck a quick glance at Officer D. "I like all these folks here, and I think most of them like me too."

Pop didn't say anything, and neither did the crowd of Three Boulderites, but G had a smile from ear to ear. Loam Moonbeam had two thumbs-up, and Officer D . . . well, I had pretty good vision and she had teardrops on her cheeks.

Pop's fingers were laced together and his thumbs were spinning.

I reached for his hand. "I know you lived here once, and I know something else too."

I turned and led him slowly toward Old Red and the three boulders: Redemption, Forgiveness, Community.

Old Red had his steely eyeballs glued on my face as me and Pop stepped toward him.

I dropped Pop's hand and said, "I'd like you to meet someone. Well, I'd like you to re-meet someone. This is Mr. . . ."

But I stopped, and I noticed for the first time that the curve of Old Red's chin was just like Pop's, except with those brownish blotches and gray beard stubble that Pop didn't have . . . yet.

"Pop, this is . . . Old Pop."

Old Pop Red Norton let out a loud, deep chuckle, one I hadn't heard from him before, but one I had heard so many times from Pop.

"Hello, Jerry," Old Pop said. "You look well."

"Thank you, sir," Pop answered.

Old Pop shook his head. "Not sir, please. Call me Red." Then he winked at me. "Or Old Pop."

Pop gazed at the three boulders, soaking in their sparkling magic, like I had done days earlier. Like Old Pop had done decades earlier.

And even though I still thought my names for those boulders were pretty great, I felt that rush of smartness inside my head again because I finally understood *all* those symbol names that Old Red had chosen so long ago.

The boulder Old Pop perched on, the one called Community, was probably the most important one. I had sat there with G. I had sat there with Old Red. I imagined every Three Boulderite had plopped on that Community boulder hundreds of times, 'cause maybe it made them feel like they belonged here . . . together. They all needed each other, 'cause it was better that way.

"Old Pop," I began, "please don't sell Three Boulders. Please." I pointed to the rocks and then the fir trees and finally the little crowd of people gathered near us. "These folks love this place, and so do you. This place keeps you healthy. You even said so at church."

Old Pop gave me a wrinkly smile.

"And I love Three Boulders too." I paused. "And, Old Pop? I want to stay here . . . with you and Officer D"—I

250

turned and gave Officer D a big grin—"and everyone standing over there—"

"Jane, we have a home in Willis. I have a job there," Pop interrupted.

"Pop, listen."

I had always gone everywhere Pop took me. I never questioned him because he was my pop and I loved him. That's the way it had always been, but it didn't have to stay that way. Twelve days in Three Boulders taught me that.

I gulped a big glob of saliva. I had to tell Pop the honest truth even though it was the hardest thing I'd ever done, harder than bombing Park Street, harder than burning my hand. "Pop," I began, "I don't think I can do just you and me anymore."

Pop was looking straight at me, but his cheeks and forehead sagged.

"I don't want to go back to Willis, where it's just us." My voice was shaky. "I want more socks. Let's stay here, Pop, where we have family."

Pop's hands wiped at his droopy eyeballs and nose, and he stood there sniffing and wiping for a long while. He didn't have any words for me. He slumped onto Community boulder next to Old Pop and he cried. He cried deeper and harder than I'd ever heard, and my heart was stretching apart like a tug-of-war.

"Oh, Jane Girl," he finally said. "My strong, sweet, smart girl . . ."

The Three Boulders crowd had silently moved closer to us.

"You deserve a mountain of socks, not just me." He stood and reached his arms out and pulled me in for another one of his sweaty chest hugs.

"I can't stay in Three Boulders," Pop continued, "because I have to get better."

"But you said you were dry again, Pop." My cheek was smooshed against his shirt.

Pop pushed me away, but he held on to my shoulders snuggly. "I am, but I want to be dry forever, and I need help with that in Willis with my counselor and sponsor."

Pop looked up and spoke to Officer D. "Doris? Will you take care of my Jane Girl? I know you've been good to her."

Officer D stepped forward. She put her beefy arm around me. "For as long as you need, Jerry."

I heard Dandy clapping.

Then Pop turned and faced Old Pop. He inhaled real deep and asked, "Red, will you watch over my Jane too? She needs family."

Old Pop gripped his crooked stick and rose from the boulder. I thought he was going to reach out and shake Pop's hand, strong and firm, but that didn't happen.

The Three Boulders crowd watched Old Red. It was like

we were all at the church fire pit, and everyone was taking a moment for prayer. I half expected a little wind gust, for God to speak to all of us, to give us important words.

But what happened was that Old Pop reached out his skinny arms and pulled Pop toward him and squeezed him like the long-lost grandson he was. And after hugging Pop for a lifetime of missed hugs, Old Pop wrapped a skinny arm around me. And soon, Officer D's burly arms joined the hug, and then G's arms, and Loam's and every other Three Boulderite arm.

I was right in the middle of that enormous group hug, and even though Pop wasn't staying with me, he was still a matching sock. But now I realized that every person in this big lump of bodies and arms was my family, and my sock drawer was big enough for all of them.

And I think Pop realized that too.

One Month Later

A New Rainbow

Old Pop didn't sell his land.

The only folks who left Three Boulders were the Carters, which made everyone a bit sad, but it did allow me and Officer D to move into the Carters' old cabin, which was only two cabins down from Old Pop.

Me and Old Pop were becoming good matching socks. I went to his cabin each day, and he always had a story for me about Three Boulders and all the people who had lived here. My favorite stories were the ones with my grandma Florence. I sure wish I had met her.

That morning, when I entered Noreen's dining hall, Loam waved his arms over his head. "Jane!" he yelled. "Come here."

I pulled out a bench and joined him and G and all the other sunshine kids. Timmy Spencer got up and moved next to me. He squeezed my arm.

"Everything's almost ready for Saturday's surprise birthday party," Loam said. "Do you think Officer Dashell suspects anything?"

"Probably. She's a good cop. But I've been using my confidentiality and I've fooled her before."

Not that I was real proud of that.

I liked calling Officer D, Officer D-Mom now. She was one of my favorite matching socks in my drawer. We had cocoa together almost every night, and I would tell her about my day and sometimes she told me about the cop stuff she handled down in Willis. She's giving me batting lessons too, but I know I'll never be as good at softball as her. I sure hoped Officer D-Mom would like our surprise.

G said, "Noreen is making Officer Dashell's favorite old-fashioned doughnuts, the confetti is cut, the banners are finished, and now we're making cards."

Dandy clapped her hands.

I knew what she was telling me. She had finished her rainbow today. I turned to the large window on the south side of the dining hall. Loam's dad and Mr. Landau had built shelves that arced over the window. Dandy's rainbow was a thing of beauty, for sure, real museum quality. Folks just started giving her items they didn't need. Sometimes she and Loam found things, but they were done stealing. Loam was conquering his ogre.

So was Pop.

I missed all the me-and-Pop good times, especially our longboarding, but I liked not worrying about the bad times.

I was proud of Pop. He was working hard at the warehouse and going to his meetings every day like he was required to do. Every Sunday, he came up to Three Boulders to visit me. On those days, Pop and Old Pop had their own private meetings. They told me I could sit with them, but I didn't. I thought they needed time and space to heal and find redemption and forgiveness and all that stuff.

One day, maybe soon, Pop could move here too, with me and all these nice folks, my new family.

But until then, me and the People of Three Boulders . . . well . . . we got this.

And that's the honest truth.

Acknowledgments

My heroes have always been authors. As a child I devoured books by Beverly Cleary and Roald Dahl. My childhood world was rocked by Mildred Taylor's *Roll of Thunder, Hear My Cry* and Katherine Paterson's *Bridge to Terabithia*. Today, there is no end to the list of children's authors who inspire me with their stories and voices. I am deeply humbled and honored to step into the community of children's literature with this novel.

My sock drawer of support for this long journey from first draft to publication is overflowing. I'm indebted to so many. I'll start at the beginning and thank my mom. Thank you for believing me when, at age seven, I told you I was going to be an author. You've been my forever cheerleader. Thank you to my dad, who is my favorite coach. Thank you for teaching me to hustle and to simply try my best. I love you both.

I am grateful to my agent, Ted Malawer, and his unending patience and willingness to travel with me. Thank you to my editor, Erica Sussman at HarperCollins, who loved Jane from the beginning and gave me just the right suggestions to make Jane's story the honest truth. Matching socks go to the talented artistic team of Abigail Dela Cruz, Jenna Stempel-Lobell, and Alison Donalty for the glorious cover.

My critique group deserves the longest standing ovation ever. Sandy Grubb, you have probably read every draft of Jane's story, and your guidance as an editor and friend is irreplaceable. Sarvinder Naberhaus, thank you for always reminding me to dig deeper. The digging was exhausting and emotional but worth it. Jill Van Den Eng, your work ethic and keen insight is more of an inspiration than you realize. Kerry McGee, thank you for your medical wisdom on signs of infection, but more so for your wisdom of story. Suzanne Klein, thank you for your ability to show me how to set a scene, and for crying along with me and Jane. Diana Schaffter, thank you for your fresh perspective and your compassion for children. I also send gratitude to other writers who read early drafts and touched this story: Holly, Ann, Stephanie, Kathy, Lori, Smadar, and Gayle.

Thank you to the staff at Jacob Wismer Elementary. It is an honor to work with such an exceptional group of educators. My students, present and past, deserve much recognition. You are why I write. Few things offer as much joy as watching your faces light up with a good book.

My extended family is enormous and quirky, and I love you all: Julie and Dan, Jack and Mary Ann, Kate, Patrice and Jordan, Joe and Ann, Alaine, Tony and Monique, Regan and Brad, and my sixteen incredible nieces and nephews and their families.

And last, yet always first in my heart, thank you to the three most important and beloved people in the world to me: Steve, Alli, and Ryan. You are *my* three boulders.

And that's the complete honest truth.